at the
CEMETERY GATES

VOLUME 2

BRHEL & SULLIVAN

CEMETERY GATES
MEDIA

At the Cemetery Gates: Volume 2
Published by Cemetery Gates Media
Binghamton, NY

ISBN: 9781728780245

For more information about this book and other Cemetery Gates Media publications, visit us at:

cemeterygatesmedia.com
facebook.com/cemeterygatesmedia
twitter.com/cemeterygatesm
instagram.com/cemeterygatesm

Cover illustration by Chad Wehrle

CONTENTS

INTRODUCTION

When we released *At the Cemetery Gates: Year One* in the fall of 2016, it was to document (and celebrate) our first year as co-writers, bringing together the finest stories that we released alongside our themed anthologies, *Tales from Valleyview Cemetery* and *Marvelry's Curiosity Shop*. To our surprise, it has gradually become one of our best reviewed books on Goodreads and Amazon.

In the fall of 2017, we had, by far, our greatest success: an illustrated book of campfire tales titled *Corpse Cold: New American Folklore*. It's fitting that we shared our finest moment to date with our oft collaborator Chad Wehrle, as he has produced the covers for *Valleyview*, *Year One*, and now this anthology. We enjoy working with other artists, but we are delighted that our brand of storytelling is most often associated with Chad's art.

Since the release of *Year One*, we've been stockpiling horror stories while also working on novels and themed anthologies—tales that we were excited to share but didn't necessarily fit within the confines of our other works. *Corpse Cold* was designed to serve as a love letter to modern folklore; *Carol for a Haunted Man* is an homage to the Christmas stories of Charles Dickens; *Her Mourning Portrait and Other Paranormal Oddities* was written at the intersection of sci-fi, dark fantasy, and paranormal romance; *Resurrection High* is a novel full of dark humor, taking place during our high school years at the tail end of the 1990s. There just wasn't enough room for tales of witchcraft, serial murder, or brushes with the undead.

At the Cemetery Gates: Volume 2 is the final resting place for these much loved, but weeded-out, spook stories. Herein you'll find common threads with our earlier anthologies—shared themes, even characters— but this book differentiates itself, in that it's more pathologically 'modern horror' than any of our prior releases. Whereas we're inclined towards storytelling that expresses the dark, the anxiety of a protagonist when faced with paranormal circumstances, even the dread of death itself—with this work we also aim to disturb...

John and Joe
October 2018

WITH THE LIGHTS OUT

When her Aunt Joan offered to let her housesit at her cabin in rural Dannemora for the weekend, Jillian jumped at the opportunity. Jillian shared a dorm suite with four other classmates at the state college in Plattsburgh, where she majored in English with a concentration in creative writing, and she'd hardly had a moment to herself in what seemed like months. A three-day stay at her aunt's cabin—just herself, her laptop, and a plethora of junk food—was just what she needed. She had spent many a memorable day there as a kid, and it held a warm place in her heart—cookouts on the back deck, jet skiing on nearby Chazy Lake. She used to love watching movies in the living room on a rainy day, where her aunt's kitten, Zinger, would curl up on her lap and fall asleep.

Aunt Joan was a moderately successful author of historical fiction, signed to a reputable publisher, which had arranged a week-long book tour to promote her latest work, *Hearts at Ticonderoga*. With her novel just hitting bookstands, she would be city-hopping every weekend. It had been over a year since Jillian had watched the cabin for her, and she Joan was pleased that her niece was willing to do it again.

Following her final class that Friday, Jillian hurriedly threw some clothes and toiletries into her backpack and was soon off. Rain beat down on her hand-me-down Nissan Rogue as she coasted through the small village of Dannemora. A thunderstorm alert startled her when it had blared from her phone; it was hard enough seeing the road in the downpour.

When she arrived at the cabin on the outskirts of town, she rushed into the house to avoid getting drenched. The first thing she did was plug her iPhone into a kitchen outlet, as it was just about dead. She was relieved to be inside the safe and familiar confines of Aunt Joan's home, and not only because of the inclement weather.

It wasn't long before she had made herself comfortable, popping a bag of popcorn, getting cozy on the couch, and taking advantage of her aunt's big-screen TV. Outside the rain continued while the forecasted thunderstorm periodically animated the dull October sky. Jillian was flipping through satellite channels, when she paused on a breaking news story on local WPTZ. A convicted murderer named Joakim Charlier had escaped that afternoon from the nearby Clinton Correctional Facility, and authorities were involved in a massive manhunt.

She was caught up in the broadcast, sprawled out on the couch, when thunder cracked outside—it was close enough she could feel it in her chest. Almost immediately, the power went out in the cabin, leaving her in the dark. She went to retrieve her phone, but it had barely charged 10% of its battery. Jillian did catch that another emergency bulletin had been sent out about the escaped convict in the region, with strict instructions of no unnecessary travel within twenty miles of Dannemora. It was only then that she grew weary of her isolation and became all too aware of her vulnerability.

She secured the front and back doors, then closed the open windows around the first floor, all while lighting her way with her dying phone. After she had made her way upstairs and into the guest bedroom, she heard a faint, whiny *meow*. She had forgotten that Joan would leave a window open for Zinger, so the cat could come in and go as he pleased. Though Zinger was just an eight-pound, moody ball of fur, Jillian felt a sudden calm at the cat's presence, a reminder that she was in a familiar place.

Jillian rushed downstairs to reopen one of the windows, then leaned out to call for the cat, while rain pattered on her head. "Zinger! Zinger! Here, kitty!"

She waited patiently for a minute then called out again, but there was no audible sign of the cat's presence. "Alright, you win! Come in when you feel like it!" Begrudgingly, she left the window open. She wasn't about to leave her aunt's sole companion out in a rainstorm all night, irrespective of runaway convicts.

Jillian went back upstairs, undressed, and got into the big, antique bed in the guest bedroom. The storm was no longer raging outside, which lessened her anxiety, though the power remained off, which wasn't surprising out in the sticks. She wanted to watch Netflix on her phone, or at least scroll through Instagram, but she knew there wasn't enough battery left for any form of entertainment. So, she plugged her phone in behind the nightstand, hoping the power would return at some point, and settled in to try and sleep.

It wasn't much past eight that evening, and she had begun drifting, as she stared at the faint outline of a wide walk-in closet, its double doors closed. She and her older sister, Steph, had made it their makeshift playroom when they were kids. They would play dress-up in their aunt's old clothes and fake jewelry, and when they were preteens they took advantage of its dark confines to tell each other scary stories inspired by their favorite TV series, *Are You Afraid of the Dark?*

Steph had told a great story about the walkup to the attic, a set of swirling stairs in the back of the closet that led to a locked trapdoor in the ceiling. It involved a ghoul named Mr. Scissors who lived behind the door and would come down at night and snip locks of hair from the sleeping girls. Steph had gotten Jillian good one night; under cover of the darkness, she managed to cut a sizeable strand of her sister's hair, and had even left a small piece of the younger girl's blonde mane on the pillow as evidence of Mr. Scissors' visit. Sure, Jillian had awoken the whole house the following morning screaming bloody murder, and their parents had grounded Steph for the remainder of the vacation, but Jillian enjoyed creepy stories, and Mr. Scissors had been one of the best she had ever heard.

Crash! Thud! Jillian was startled awake when she heard two distinct items striking the floor downstairs. She sat up, grasping the comforter to her chest, listening for further evidence of an intruder. When she heard nothing more than her own, heavy breathing, she sighed, realizing that Zinger must have come in and knocked something over.

The rain was a mere drizzle over the roof shingles as Jillian got out of bed and tiptoed downstairs, again lighting her way with her dying phone. "Zinger? Where are you, buddy?" She looked around the rustic living room, the dull light reflecting off the polished wood of the cabin.

"Oh, you made such a mess!" said Jillian, finding the toppled end table and smashed vase near the window she had left open. She called out a few more times, curious what the cat was up to, before shutting the window and returning to bed.

It was now late, and Jillian easily fell into a deep sleep, knowing Zinger had come in from the storm. She was dreaming of boating around Chazy Lake with her sister—she hadn't seen Steph since the summer and missed spending time with her—when she was painfully awoken by something biting her hand, which she had left dangling off the side of the bed.

"*Rawrr!*" snarled the creature from beneath the bed as Jillian pulled her hand up.

"*Zinger!* What the hell?!" said Jillian. But she didn't have time to process the abrupt assault, as she spied the silhouette of a large man watching her from the bedroom doorway.

"Who's there..." Jillian didn't get to finish, as the man lunged at her in bed. She tried to wriggle herself away from him as they twisted in the blankets. She kicked and hit him as hard as she could, but the larger man overpowered her.

Jillian was struggling in his grasp, when he suddenly released her arm and screamed something awful. This was followed immediately by the sound of a hissing cat. She managed to slide off the side of the bed and onto the floor while the intruder was distracted, and she had the presence of mind to grab her phone before running from the room and downstairs.

Jillian heard the man scrambling upstairs while she searched in the dark for her backpack, which held her car keys. She knew the intruder would be on her in no time, and when she found her bag she tore out the front door and got into her car, immediately hitting the power locks. She quickly located her keys under the dome light, then started her car, illuminating the intruder with her headlights as he emerged from the house. He was wearing what she assumed to be a prison jumpsuit, but couldn't really concentrate on him, as she was backing out of the narrow, rocky driveway and onto the rural highway.

Before Jillian had even considered calling the sheriff's department, she spotted the flashing lights of a police checkpoint, only a mile or so from her aunt's cabin. She pulled up with her window down and was trying not to babble at the deputies, who had circled her car with their shotguns and pistols drawn. "The escaped con is around my aunt's house! 343 Varin Road!" yelled Jillian. "He attacked me!"

The deputies got her out of the car to hear her whole story, while two cars were immediately sent off from the road block, tearing down the rural road. It was a whirlwind for her as she recounted her evening and was then whisked away to the sheriff's office by a deputy.

Jillian was given a change of clothes and a cup of hot coffee before she had a minute to call her aunt with the news.

"Hey, Jillian! Is the power out?" asked Joan as soon as she picked up.

"Yes!" said Jillian. "Have you heard about the escape from Dannemora yet?"

"Gosh, no! Lock the doors, dear!"

"It's too late, Aunt Joan," said Jill, nearly out of breath with all she had to tell her aunt. "I'm safe now, at the sheriff's office. But the convict was inside the cabin!"

Jillian recounted the details of the storm and power outage, of leaving the window open for the cat and her narrow escape from the murderer.

"Oh my goodness, Jilly," said Joan. "But it doesn't make any sense..."

"What doesn't make sense?"

"My Zinger died months ago. Killed by a coyote, I think," said Joan. "He's buried in the backyard. I figured your mother would've told you..."

"What do you mean *he's dead*. He probably saved my life tonight."

"Jill, you're breaking up..."

Jillian looked down at her phone. It had finally shut off, the battery completely drained. She thought about her night, what her aunt had said about Zinger being long dead. But she had heard him outside and then beneath the bed—hadn't she?

Her thoughts were interrupted by a line of sodden police officers, escorting two men in handcuffs. She didn't get a good look at either of them, as they were marched through the open office and into a backroom.

There was plenty of commotion in the office, phones ringing, people shouting orders back and forth regarding the capture. When things finally calmed down, the deputy that had driven Jillian into town returned.

"Miss, I know tonight has been pretty intense for you..." said Deputy Kent.

"What's wrong?" She had immediately detected his hesitancy to tell her something.

"We captured the man we were looking for, not far from your aunt's cabin," said Kent. "But we also picked up another man while searching—inside the cabin."

"There were two escapees?" asked Jillian.

"No. We're actually not sure who this other guy is, and my captain wants you to try and identify who attacked you."

The thought of it gave her goosebumps. She didn't know if she could look into the eyes of a murderer. The puzzle of the mysterious second man barely registered with her at the time.

"I guess I could, if it's really necessary..." said Jillian, quietly.

Minutes later she was taken back to a hallway with a series of windowed interview rooms. On one side was the large, bearded man in the jumpsuit, whom she knew to be her attacker. It didn't take a moment for her to identify him. She was relieved that he didn't even look up at her during the brief process. It was just a window; it wasn't like a police lineup with two-way mirrors, something you might see on TV.

However, she was confused by the second man she was asked to identify. He was sallow-looking, slight, probably not even five-feet-tall—and he didn't take his eyes off her. This other man had long, stringy hair and jaundiced eyes that seemed to be all sclera, with only a little black for irises and pupils. She could hear his teeth chattering through the glass. He was soaked to the bone, just staring through her, past her—perhaps into her past?

The hand on her shoulder startled her. "Miss, have you seen this man before?" asked Kent.

She didn't immediately reply. He seemed very familiar, though she knew she had never *seen* him before.

"Jillian, did this man attack you too?" said Kent. "It's probable that Charlier had someone helping him on the outside..."

"No. I've never seen him," said Jillian. "Where did you say they found him?"

"He was hiding in a large closet on the second floor of your aunt's cabin," said Kent.

Jillian couldn't help but stare back at the pasty man, transfixed. Without a word, he raised his hands and made scissor motions into the air, which seemed to send Jillian cascading through her memories, back to her girlhood frights. It rekindled a very specific terror that her sister's stories had brought about in her, a feeling that she had learned to enjoy, and would eventually relish. The man smiled broadly at her, showing his ugly, yellow-stained teeth, and then mewled like a cat—like a very familiar cat.

THE PAYPHONE

I used to walk to school with my sister and a few of the neighborhood kids. Most days we walked to school and back without stopping. In the morning we were usually running behind, so we couldn't mess around. The walk home was different, though; there was time to stop at the baseball card store, or the pharmacy for ten-cent candy. Sometimes we would take longer, alternate routes home, up the hill and then back down to our neighborhood. But usually we were excited to get to our babysitter's house to play Nintendo, or to read to each other from a new book of scary stories we had just taken out from the school library. On our afternoon walks there was plenty of time for us to pull pranks, get in fights with other kids, commit petty acts of vandalism, and trespass. But making pranks calls from the payphone at the vacant corner store was one of our favorite pastimes.

There was an empty lot that we walked through on our trek to school. It was our private playground in that span of time between leaving school and our babysitter's expectation of our arrival. We had snowball fights there, played tag, dumped the sewer grate into the sewer, hoping a car would get stuck in the square hole—I didn't say we were good kids. So, it was inevitable that we would mess with the payphone as soon as we were tall enough to properly dial numbers. We had seen Bart Simpson do it enough on our favorite cartoon and video game and wanted in on the action.

My sister Jenny would save a quarter from her lunch money specifically to use at the payphone. We knew that our phone number was like other numbers in our area, so we would usually punch in '7-2-9' followed by four other random digits, repeating until we got someone, or at least an answering machine. It seemed like it was usually an older man who'd answer, which made sense because it was 3:30 in the middle of the week. The typical prank call would go:

"Hello?" An old, gruff voice would come over the handset.

"Hi, this is April O'Neil from Channel 6 News," said Jenny.

"Channel what now?"

"Have you seen the Shredder in your neighborhood?"

"The Shredder? What are you talking about, kid?"

"How about Bebop or Rocksteady?"

"Listen, you better get your dad on the phone, right now!"

"My dad will kick the shit out of you!"

The old guys would usually start losing it, cursing and threatening a 10-year-old girl. Jenny loved getting strong reactions from adults, and we'd all laugh as we ran the rest of the way home.

Eventually, we figured out we could call '800' and '900' numbers and not have to pay anything to get some poor salesman or customer service person over the phone. We'd call Jenny Craig, memorable infomercial numbers, pizza shops, vending machine companies, anything we saw advertised that we could remember.

We never dialed the operator directly, as our mother had warned us The Operator knew all and would send a policeman to our house if we ever called her. I was afraid of the operator, even when we were making our prank calls from the payphone. Every now and then, we'd dial a non-existent number and get the operator. I would usually apologize and tell her I dialed the wrong number, but my sister was different. She would get to talking to the operator, trying to figure out if she knew where we were. Jenny was trying to verify or debunk our mother's warning.

"Joey, she doesn't know where we are. Mom's nuts," said Jenny, after hanging up the payphone one afternoon. "Let's call her back and ask her if she knows a good refrigerator repairman."

"Let's just go home. I don't wanna prank the operator."

"You're such a wuss. You really think she's gonna send a cop to arrest two kids for making prank calls?" Jenny hit the '0' and put the phone to her ear.

I backed away, ready to run and catch up with the babysitter's kids, who had gotten sick of messing with the payphone.

"Hello, I'm looking for a good refrigerator repairman."

I couldn't make out what the operator replied.

"My refrigerator won't stop running, and I can barely keep up with it!" said Jenny, laughing into the phone.

A moment later she dropped the receiver. "Ouch!"

"What?!" I asked, watching the phone dangle.

"She buzzed me," replied Jenny, sticking her finger in her ear.

"Huh?"

"She didn't like my joke, so she played this irritating tone."

I snickered, that the operator had given her a taste of her own medicine, and we headed to the babysitter's.

A few days later, Jenny thought she had a great joke for the operator. She was sore that the woman had gotten her and wanted to get the woman back. I didn't know exactly what she had planned, but she made me take my trumpet out of its case.

"Joey, I'm gonna get the lady on the phone and you blast her as loud as you can with your trumpet."

It all made me nervous. There were still people driving by who would certainly think twice about two kids standing at a payphone holding a trumpet. "I don't want to, Jenny. We'll get in trouble."

"Do it! You won't get in trouble, anyway. I will." She was older, and much bigger than me. I didn't like getting beat by her, so ultimately it didn't take much for me to raise my trumpet, ready to blow into the phone as she got the operator on the phone.

"Hi, I'm looking for an instrument repair shop. My horn is way too loud!" Jenny nodded to me, then turned the receiver in my direction. I hesitated, but she gave me her patented hostile stare, so I blew into the mouthpiece with everything I had. I surprised myself, and Jenny, with the volume I was able to produce.

A car had stopped nearby, so Jenny grabbed my trumpet case, and I held my instrument as we ran through the lot, all the way to our babysitter's house. When we were safely inside, we couldn't stop laughing, replaying how the operator must have reacted—falling off her chair, her headset flying off her head—for the rest of the afternoon.

The following day, Jenny and I were walking home by ourselves. She couldn't help herself. I tried to pull her away from the payphone, but she pushed me away.

"Frankie says relax, Joey. I'm just gonna check up on our friend. Maybe she's on a sick day because her brain got rattled."

"Please, Jenny, let's forget about it. We're really gonna get in trouble if we keep messing with the phone company." I began walking away. It was too risky for me.

I looked over my shoulder, hoping she would follow, but she already had the phone up to her ear. I kept walking, looking back, anticipating a cop car pulling in with its lights flashing, ready to arrest my sister.

I didn't hear anything when it happened, but I did see her collapse. I rushed back to where she lay motionless, and I was as terrified as I'd ever been, because of the way in which she had simply crumpled to the asphalt.

"Jenny! Jenny, get up!" I shook her as the payphone dangled above my head. I could hear a strange tone emanating from it, which shifted pitches depending on the direction the phone was swinging.

Moments later Jenny's eyes opened wide. She looked up at me dazed, as if she had no idea where she was, or what had just happened. I helped her up and she didn't say anything, then I saw a trickle of blood coming from her right ear.

"Your ear! There's blood coming from it!" I pointed to her ear, and she still looked wildly confused.

"What?" Jenny slowly placed her finger to her ear and then looked at it, studying the blood, trying to figure out what had occurred.

She then looked me in the eye, holding the right side of her head. I'd never seen her that vulnerable, or scared.

"Joey, I can't hear!"

KARA FINDS HER MATCH

Kara Lazar lived alone in a little, brick, two-bedroom house beside a rural cemetery. She was already thirty-six but still planning on meeting the right guy and starting a family. Unfortunately for Kara, she was terrible at first dates. She put too much pressure on the situation, was too judgmental of her prospective partners, and could use a brush-up in manners and common decency.

There was a bar across the street from her house, and a gas station within sight of her front stoop, but not much else within walking distance—except for pasture and forest. She could jog the cemetery grounds in peace, and could usually convince men to meet her for a drink at the Octagon Bar and Grill nearby. She took pride in the fact that men were still willing to drive out of their way just to have a drink with her. Kara preferred the quiet hamlet of Newfield to the bustling commercial center of Ithaca, New York, where she worked as a secretary in Cornell's biochemistry department. Plus, she could afford a house in the countryside; Ithaca's rents were sky-high for upstate New York.

Living away from the city made it difficult to meet new people, although she garnered plenty of attention on dating sites and apps. Lynette, her boss and one close friend, had set her up with a guy named Chris, a graduate student whom Kara had only seen in passing.

"Just tell him to text me when he gets to the Octagon," said Kara.

Lynette sighed. "He's really a great guy. You should call him and chat with him at lunch."

"Lyn, no one calls a guy they don't know for a chat!"

Lynette laughed. "You have so many rules you live by. I hope you give him a real chance."

"It's just a drink," said Kara. "No dinner, no appetizers."

"I already told him not to embarrass me."

"Good. Some guys are just way too forward and try and say too much."

That evening Kara got her first text from Chris, which merely stated: "I'm at the Octagon Bar. Hope to see you soon!"

Kara put her iPhone face down on her bathroom sink and continued to do her hair and makeup. She already knew he wasn't going to work out. She could feel it in her gut. He was still a student at thirty-five.

Twenty minutes later Kara stepped through the door at the Octagon. She smiled at Chris and he waved, appearing unperturbed by her late entrance. He stood and she half-hugged him, using her purse to prevent too much contact. They sat together at the bar and she ordered a white wine. The fact that he already had a half-finished beer in front of him didn't bode well.

"Sorry I'm late!" she said.

"No worries. You look great!" said Chris.

Kara could tell he was nervous. She didn't like when a guy was too nervous, because then he wouldn't say enough, or would say the wrong things.

"Did you have any trouble finding the bar?"

"I did take a wrong turn. The GPS isn't very accurate out here," said Chris. "Plus, service is spotty."

"Yep, I love it out here!"

Kara and Chris sipped their drinks and looked around the bar, each too nervous to start the conversation. A group was huddled around the dart-board, a man and woman were playing pool, and a couple of old-timers were chugging beers at the other end of the bar while the Mets got clobbered by the Dodgers.

"So, you live nearby?" asked Chris.

"Yes." Kara wasn't going to tell him she lived right across the street.

"Is this one of your regular hangouts?"

She considered any implication. Did he think she was low-class? A drunk? Why would he phrase it like that?

"Not really. But I prefer it to the Collegetown bars when school's in session."

"Not a big fan of students?" Chris grinned.

"Spoiled kids who rely on Mommy and Daddy for everything, while they play at 'being adult,' grate at me, frankly."

Chris' face flushed at her sudden showing of snobbery. "Where did you go to college?"

She finished the last of her wine and pretended not to hear his question. Chris was cute, but not cute enough to continue into the first-date questions that she had long grown bored of.

"Nice meeting you, Chris." She smiled broadly at him while standing and dropping a ten on the bar. "But I've got to do my laundry and a few other chores."

He gave her a half-hearted 'bye' then returned to his beer.

Kara returned home and put on her comfy clothes, then sat on her couch with a wine in one hand and her phone in the other. She swiped left on one guy after another. They seemed too young, too old, too divorced, too bearded, too conservative, too vegan. She was about to switch apps when she decided to try and narrow her search results for a gag, to only see guys *outside* of Ithaca.

She found a few farmers, a couple construction guys, no one particularly interesting, but lingered over the profile of a well-dressed forty-year-old named Kevin. He hadn't been active on the dating service in months, and was likely already in a relationship, but she swiped right on him anyway. Kara then finished her drink and then went to bed. She was over dating, for the rest of the weekend, anyway.

"I can't believe you told him you had to do laundry!" said Lynette. It was Monday morning and Kara was back at the office, ready for Lynette's chastisement.

"He made me too nervous because *he* was too nervous," said Lynette. "And he just came across a lot younger than I was expecting."

"Kara, he said he spent more time *waiting for you* than you actually spent with him."

"I'm sorry, Lyn. Just tell him I'm a flake." She knew Lynette was genuinely upset with her and felt bad.

"I'm not going to tell him that."

"It's *so* hard finding a boyfriend," said Kara. "I'm either too old for them or they have too many kids by now."

"You don't give these guys a chance. It's like you're already looking over their shoulder as soon as you meet up with them," said Lynette. "There won't always be a line of quality men trying to get a date with you."

Kara was at home one morning, sitting in her window seat facing the cemetery, with her coffee. She watched as a tall man walked along the paths of the graveyard. He looked businesslike, and had a long, confident stride.

She put her coffee down and hurried up to her room to change into her workout clothes. She was going for a jog.

Soon, Kara was made up, wearing her most attractive yoga pants and halter top out on the cemetery paths. She wanted to get a better look at the guy. On her first pass she smiled coyly at him, and he smiled back. She thought he looked familiar but couldn't quite place him. On her second pass she smiled broadly, and again he smiled back. She stopped dead in her tracks. It was the man she had found on Tinder the night of her crappy first date with Chris!

The man must've noticed that she stopped because he, too, stopped. He turned to greet her, but she spoke first: "Hey, you look familiar. Do you live around here?"

"Yeah. My name's Kevin."

She already knew that. They took a few steps closer to each other. Both seemed drawn to the other. It was the most natural first meeting that Kara had ever experienced. "I'm Kara."

They chatted briefly, he made her laugh. She was so caught up in the moment that she almost forgot she had to be to work. "I'm sorry, I've got to get going, Kevin. Would you wanna meet up for a drink at the Octagon later?"

"How about eight?" said Kevin.

"I'll see you then."

Kara was ecstatic. Meeting the one Tinder guy that she had found intriguing in-person and hitting it off with him—it felt like fate. She couldn't wait to tell

Lynette about Kevin when she got to the office that morning.

"You made a date with a guy you met in the *cemetery?*" asked Lynette.

"I technically saw his profile on Tinder first," said Kara.

"Did he see yours?"

"Possibly, but he didn't swipe right on me."

"I have no idea what that means," said Lynette, who was ten years her senior. "I'm wondering whether it's possible that he's stalking you?"

"*Ha, no!* If anything, I was stalking *him* from my window."

"I hope it works out for you, Kara. Just don't get ahead of yourself before you have a real date with him."

"I really think he's what I'm looking for," said Kara. "There's just something that makes sense about him."

"Let me know how it goes, dear."

Kara was showered and ready by 7:30 that evening. She wasn't going to make Kevin wait. She even arrived at the Octagon a few minutes before eight, which was totally unlike her. She wasn't surprised when Kevin arrived right at eight. He didn't seem like the overeager type.

"Hi!" Kara got up and hugged him. She liked his cologne. She noticed he was wearing the same blue suit as that morning, but she figured he was coming from work.

"What do you drink?" he asked.

"White wine."

Kevin ordered her a wine and a beer for himself, and they sat at a small table in the corner and got to know each other.

"This might be the best first date I've ever been on, Kevin."

He smiled. "I was really looking forward to meeting up with you."

"Gosh, I hope you got some work done today," she flirted.

"I practically ran here!"

They laughed. He took her hand. She flinched when she saw the amount of dirt beneath his longish nails. She couldn't believe such an immaculately groomed man would let his hands go unchecked. But she stopped herself from recoiling and commenting on his one outward flaw, considering all the things Lynette had been telling her about her unrealistic expectations.

It was a little after eleven and they were both buzzing from their conversation and mutual attraction, along with the copious amount of alcohol that they had consumed.

"You should come over. I live across the street," said Kara, staring at the handsome catch who sat across the table.

"Okay. Let's go," beamed Kevin.

He paid the tab and they glided across the street to Kara's place, hand in hand. They were barely through the threshold when she pounced on him. They kissed against the coat rack, made out in the parlor, and slowly undressed on their way up to Kara's bedroom.

"I can't believe this is happening," whispered Kara as she and Kevin embraced in her bed.

"You're perfect," said Kevin.

Kara's thoughts raced in the dark room as Kevin slept soundly beside her. She wondered what he would think of her now. The fact that they had only met that morning and she had already slept with him. It really wasn't how she would want to come across to a prospective boyfriend. She began to have serious doubts about the viability of their fledgling relationship.

Kara slowly got out of bed and went to the bathroom. She stared at her mussed hair and streaky makeup in the mirror and assumed the worst. Kevin wouldn't think that she was someone to take seriously; he might just consider her a hookup. She stayed in the guest bedroom for the rest of the night, planning out how she would handle him in the morning.

"Hey, Kev," Kara called softly as she entered her bedroom.

He was facing away. She sat on the bed next to him. "Kevin, sorry to wake you, but I have to get to work."

He didn't stir. When she put her hand on his exposed shoulder to rustle him from sleep, she shuddered. He was cold to the touch.

"Kevin!" She shook him, but he didn't wake.

When she pulled him over onto his back she screamed. His eyes had rolled back into his head and he was an odd, pallid color. Kara didn't know CPR or anything useful, so she called 911 and waited on her front stoop for the EMTs to arrive.

A volunteer firefighter and a sheriff's deputy were the first to show. She led them to the bedroom but didn't enter. They raced in and got to work. Kara went back outside to direct the EMTs to the room only minutes later. The emergency personnel gathered in her bedroom talked quietly while she paced in the hall. She made sure to text Lynette about what had happened, letting her know the intimate details of her night.

She caught a few of the comments from the other room. 'He's long gone' was all she could focus on. She kicked herself for sleeping in the other room. Maybe she could have heard him struggling and contacted someone sooner. How did it happen? Did he have a heart attack? She couldn't comprehend it—she had finally found the perfect man then lost him just like that.

The deputy and an EMT walked her downstairs and outside to talk to her.

"Ma'am, did you say he was fine last night?" asked the deputy.

"Yes! He was the picture of health," said Kara.

The medic wheeled out the stretcher.

"Ma'am, the medics are going to take you to the ER, just to be safe," said the deputy.

"I'm fine," said Kara. "Why would I need to go to the ER? Do you think he had something that I might've caught?!"

"That's what I'm thinking," said the deputy.

Kara let the EMT strap her onto the stretcher and push her into the back of the ambulance. "Gosh, this is tight. I can't even move my arms to itch my nose."

"It's for your safety, ma'am."

The other EMT appeared and closed the doors on Kara. He drove them to the hospital and wheeled Kara into the emergency room. They placed her in her own room and she waited, still secured to the stretcher. Eventually, a woman in a lab coat came in and sat in a chair beside her.

"Hello, I'm Dr. Nabokov. I run the psychiatric unit here. Is there anyone I can contact on your behalf?"

"Psychiatric unit?! What am I doing here?"

"I'm sorry, Kara," said Dr. Nabokov. "We're going to admit you for observation."

"What are you talking about? What right do you have to do so? Let me up, this is ridiculous!" screeched Kara, struggling on the stretcher.

"Law allows me to admit necrophiliacs, grave-robbers, folks who store or fail to report corpses in their place of residence."

"Huh?! Kevin *just* died!" screamed Kara. "I didn't sleep with him when he was dead! That's sick! I actually spent the night in the guest bedroom."

"You met a sheriff's deputy earlier?"

"Yeah. So?"

"I just got off the phone with him. He says he and a firefighter found a disturbed grave in the cemetery that adjoins your house," said Dr. Nabokov. "Did you dig a man up and place him in your bed?"

"No! I was at the bar with Kevin last night! Ask the bartender or any of the regulars. They know me."

"Kara, the medics didn't bother to work on the man in your bed this morning because he was already embalmed. He's been dead for months."

Kara couldn't fathom it. She raged, struggling to move against the straps that secured her. What sort of sick joke were they pulling? Why had Kevin died during the night? Were they covering up his death? Did he have some mysterious illness that they weren't telling her about? Then it hit her like a punch to the gut. His dirty nails.

"His nails are dirty! Look at his nails! He must've clawed his way out of his grave yesterday morning!"

The doctor let her rave on, make empty threats, then beg and plead for her release, but she was soon admitted to the wing for the especially deranged.

MIXTAPE: HALLOWEEN '84

I arrived at my father's doorstep on a crisp fall evening, having not spoken to him in years. We had little in common, beyond our shared occupation, and there likely wasn't all that much time to work on our relationship as it was. My father had left me a voicemail a few months prior, that he had been diagnosed with advanced prostate cancer and didn't know if he'd survive it. I didn't call him back at the time.

The man—Alonzo Ribeiro—had cheated on my mother, left us high and dry after she kicked him out of the house, and he only took me in when I was a teenager because she had passed away. Needless to say, those were some intense years. I regret many of the things I said to my father as a seventeen-year-old, but I don't regret breaking contact with him once I came of age.

Alonzo was a toxic father and the antithesis of a family man—a detective married to his job. Not that it mattered that he was always working, since he was a chronic cheater, and rarely bothered concealing his improprieties. He tortured my mother, but she and I got away from him and we had a great time of it for the eight or so years between my parents' divorce and her car wreck.

"Detective James Ribeiro!" said Alonzo, opening the front door, though I hadn't rung or knocked yet.

I couldn't help but cringe at the inflection he placed on 'detective.' A major point of contention after I'd graduated high school was whether I'd enter the police academy or get a degree in criminal justice before entering the academy. At no point was it ever a possibility that I'd go to college and entertain the prospects of a career outside of law enforcement.

So, I sought my own way in the world, paying for my own school and working full-time to not have to deal with my father's demands, and it worked out well. I graduated with a degree in business, found myself a good job with a financial company. But then the Financial Crisis of 2008 hit, and my firm went under.

After I was laid off there was only one organization interested in what Jimmie, son of Alonzo Ribeiro, had to offer the world. I graduated from the police academy, excelled as an officer, and eventually made detective.

"Hey, Dad. How's retirement?"

"Come in, Jimmie. We'll get to all that," said Alonzo.

I shrugged and followed him inside. We sat at his dining room table. The house was a mess. He'd relied on girlfriends all along to take care of his homes and apartments. It looked like he hadn't had a woman around for quite some time.

"You brought the case?"

"Yep, it's all here," I said, opening a series of yellowed manila folders.

My father briefly looked over the paperwork and the old Polaroids of the brutal crime scenes, before pushing them aside. I figured he'd gone over them so many times during his career that he was anaesthetized to the violence they depicted.

"Do they have the younger guys doing history reports now?" said Alonzo.

"Yeah, it's standard practice all over the country now," I replied. "Going over cold cases is not only solid procedural training, but these sorts of cases are being reopened..."

"This case *was* solved," blurted Alonzo. "We got the guy on drug charges, instead of murder."

"Why is there no evidence tying Kevin Tripp to any of the murder scenes then?"

My father shook his head. "Kevin Tripp was the Toolbox Torturer. He was a proven serial rapist and after we put him away the murders stopped."

"Dad, there are countless cases of serial rapists and murderers who go dormant for years, decades even. Just look at the Golden State Killer..."

My father slapped the table, scattering a few of the pictures. I couldn't help but flinch. "You'll learn, Jimmie. Nothing is ever as cut and dry as you want it to be," said Alonzo. "You see the pictures, read the reports, but you weren't there. You didn't smell the blood in the junkyard or see the decayed, abused bodies of these women. A man who could do that—someone that sadistic—doesn't just figure out how to control his sick impulses."

"Alright, I get it," I said. I didn't want to get him worked up. I wasn't there to piss him off. I just wanted to go over the timeline of the investigation with him.

"You will someday, son," said Alonzo. "We didn't have the technology to pin these guys down with DNA. There weren't cameras and audio rolling everywhere, all the time. But we still caught the bad guys."

"Relax, Dad," I said. "I'm not here to grill you about the *Die Hard*, cowboy cop stuff you guys had to do to get..."

He stood abruptly. "We couldn't just sit at our computers and send emails all day. We had to be out in the street, talking to the pimps and dealers, making hard deals for information."

"Yeah, you guys had a tougher time of it," I said. "I'm not saying that you didn't spend long hours out on the streets. I should know, better than most. You were never around when I was a kid."

His face deflated. I hadn't meant to say that last bit. The man was exasperating, and it was still so easy for me to needle him whenever he left an opening. I was surprised when he didn't snap back at me with an insult.

"Jimmie, let's just get back to the case."

We went over the timeline of events. The first body discovered in the forest behind the junkyard in Elmdale. A local girl, her life ended by a screwdriver through the ear. I felt nauseous when my father described how it had been driven into her head with a rock. The pictures really didn't do the scene justice.

"So, you guys found another mutilated body in the creek, just a mile from the junkyard, and a few months later is when Susan Greer was discovered inside the van, within the junkyard itself?"

His eyes darted around, I could only assume he was flipping through a Rolodex of memories he'd long since buried. "Yes. That sounds right," said Alonzo, scraping one of the faded Polaroids over his thumb. "Susan was tore up. My God. He'd gone at her woman parts with needle-nose pliers... I still can't imagine how no one heard her scream."

"Dad, the evidence list has a cassette tape on it," I said, trying to get him back on task. "It's the only thing I couldn't find in the evidence locker. Do you remember anything about it?"

Again, he went to his Rolodex. I just assumed he wouldn't remember it. "Yeah, we found a tape in the van."

"What was on it?"

"I think it was just an unmarked tape," said Alonzo. "But I do remember that we lost it."

I couldn't help but chuckle. "So, losing evidence wasn't a big deal in the Eighties?"

He practically snarled at me. "We swept it for prints. It was a cassette tape in a junkyard."

"Did you listen to the tape yourself?"

"Yeah, I took it home to analyze," said Alonzo. "I was the one who lost it."

"Again, wasn't losing evidence frowned upon, even back then?" I was trying to make light of it and was surprised that my father didn't crack a smile.

"It was the day your mother kicked me out."

I hadn't expected that. "I was staying overnight at Rob Batdorf's house..."

"It's good you weren't there," said Alonzo. "She really let me have it, threw my stuff on the front lawn. The tape sorta got lost in the fray."

I waited for him to continue. I'd never heard either of my parents talk about the details of that night.

"She found a few motel charges on my Visa statement," said Alonzo. "I could never lie to her. I could cheat on her and treat her like dirt, but I could never lie to her face."

He stopped short of crying. "I really screwed up, Jimmie."

"We don't have to get into it, Dad. It was a long time ago. I'm just trying to figure out if you listened to the tape from the evidence list..."

"I don't remember," said Alonzo, following a pregnant pause. "It must've been terrible for your mother and you. I wish I could go back…"

"I'm over it, Dad."

"Christ. That girl's scream. I still dream about it," said Alonzo. "I don't know how nobody heard her."

"There was something on the tape, then?" I asked, my curiosity piqued.

"He told her what he was going to do to her. He taunted her," said Alonzo. "She didn't say much, but she definitely knew him."

"He recorded her murder?"

"Not the murder. The torture," said Alonzo, gulping. I could tell he was reeling inside, reliving countless murder scenes. "He would taunt her, and he was so calm about it. He'd tell her she wasn't screaming loud enough, that if she screamed loud enough he'd stop. You could hear him whacking her with the hammer, pulling at her body with the pliers…"

His description of what he'd heard sent my thoughts spiraling thirty years into the past. Through fragments of my childhood, where nostalgia patches together the best of times and glosses over every bad memory short of the traumatic. *I had heard the torture tape!*

I got up from the table and rushed to my father's attic. I knew he never threw anything away. It would still be up there. A box of cassettes from the mid-Eighties that had been passed over during countless garage sales. Movie soundtracks, obscure children's tapes, but more importantly, my mixtapes.

I rummaged through the area of the attic that held my past. Old board games, broken toys, notebooks, the sort of junk I'd left behind for good when I moved out at eighteen. I found my old cassette recorder first. It brought back a flood of memories—sitting by the radio, waiting for a specific song to add to my latest mixtape.

There were countless mixtapes, but I labeled them all. I knew exactly which one I was looking for. *Halloween '84*. I'd listened to it countless times, having found it in a box of my father's junk not long after he moved out. I'd collected other Halloween tapes. Hallmark had one that I loved, full of atmospheric, spooky sounds. They all had screaming, torture, rattling chains, etc.—I'm sure you couldn't find a kids' recording like that in the Hallmark Store these days.

Every October I listened to those horror tapes. I even had a haunted house in the basement one year. It makes my skin crawl to think about it now, since *Halloween '84* was my go-to soundtrack when I invited the neighborhood kids over. Having them walk through the basement in the dark with the sounds of that poor lady screaming was frightening enough. I swear Jenny Kent pissed her pants because of it.

My father was pacing around the dining room table when I returned, cassette and player in hand.

"Why'd you run up to the attic like that?" he asked.

"Sit down, Dad."

I plugged the tape player into the outlet and inserted *Halloween '84*. When I hit 'play' the chorus of the 1984 Ray Parker Jr. smash hit "Ghostbusters" blared out of the small speaker.

My father laughed then finally sat down. I didn't laugh. I panicked, thinking that I might've recorded over a missing piece of decades-old evidence. When I took the tape out I realized my error. I had the wrong side down. The A-side was labeled, in my 8-year-old scrawl, 'Spook House Sounds.'

"I found this tape when I was a kid," I said, as I flipped the cassette over and reinserted it.

When I pressed 'play' I heard the familiar static of a basic recorder, much like the one that I'd owned. You could hear some shuffling about, then the sound of tools clanking together.

"You shouldn't cry," came a gravelly voice from the speaker.

I looked at my father; he was stunned. I could tell he knew exactly what he was hearing.

A woman whimpered, she may have been crying. I could hear her labored breaths as things were shifted about.

Then the screaming began. The piercing, soul shattering howls. They were unlike anything I'd ever heard in any movie or TV show, or on my schlocky spook sound tapes. That's why it had been my most-played Halloween mixtape as a kid. It was uniquely terrifying to listen to.

"Turn it off, Jimmie." My father said it barely above a whisper during one of the lulls in the screaming.

"Can I- can I pray before you kill me?" said the victim. Her torturer answered her only by hitting her. There would be a *thump* followed by a guttural *hmmph* from the woman, which would eventually turn into more screams, and squealing pleas.

"Jimmie, the case is closed," said Alonzo, struggling to get to his feet. "Burn that wretched tape."

My father stood over me, but I didn't move to stop the recording. "Give it a minute. I've listened to this tape so many times, but I've never *really* listened to it until now," I said, transfixed on what was happening to that poor girl, in a van, in the town junkyard, decades ago.

"You don't have to," whimpered the woman, once there was another lull in the torture. *"I'm ready to die... Just let me say a prayer..."* I didn't catch all of what she

said—she was practically whispering—so I paused the tape and rewound a few seconds.

"Turn the fucking thing *off!*" yelled Alonzo.

He startled me, but he didn't make any move to take the tape player away from me. He just hovered nearby, gaunt from his illness, looking incredibly feeble for his age. I was too involved with the tape to care what his problem was.

I hit play, twisting the volume knob to ten.

"You don't have to. I'm ready to die, Lonzo," she said. *"Just let me say a prayer for you."*

The tone was so eerily familiar. How I had heard countless women call him by his nickname—how my mother had spoken it at one time: Lonzo. So tenderly; lover to lover.

SPICE OF LIFE

"Ms. Olsen, you're sagging!" chirped Wendy, the lithe, 22-year-old yoga instructor.

Nichole Olsen's body shook as she attempted to correct her form in the Downward-Facing Dog Pose that everyone else in her morning yoga class was executing so effortlessly. The entire 45-minute session had been a struggle for the 30-year-old, who had originally signed up to shed the pounds she had put on since the birth of her son. In the three months that she had attended the class, and while also seemingly starving herself, she had only managed to lose three pounds, and she still struggled to contort her soft, pear-shaped body into the most novice of poses.

"Hands flat!" barked the young commandant of the yoga room.

Now embarrassed, and already dreadfully self-conscious around the other seasoned yoga students and their vibrant instructor, Nichole took to her knees to chug from her water bottle. She avoided making eye contact with Wendy, afraid of further chastisement, as she pulled back her sweaty mop of brown hair.

Nichole's social life certainly hadn't improved since joining the Sure-Fit Athletics Club. She was desperate to converse with someone other than her five-year-old son and her often-absent husband. But it quickly became clear to her that she didn't belong: every other woman in the class (some ten to twenty years her senior) was already fit, athletic, and seemed to possess a youthful energy that had long since drained from her.

When Wendy released the class, Nichole would always be first to the locker room—as she had nobody to mill about and chat with. She would dress in an empty corner, out of everyone's way, and would listen enviously as the other women discussed their more glamorous lives and made plans for "girls' nights" and mimosa-infused playdates. It genuinely felt to her that they were completely unaware of her dowdy existence.

With hours to spare before her son returned home from school, Nichole decided to visit the Elmdale Mall. Shopping was a great comfort to her; picking up something nice for the house, or even a new pair of shoes, distracted her from her lonely, monotonous existence.

She was leaving the soap store, pleased that she had picked up the latest fall-scented foaming hand soaps and lotions, when she noticed a new business had taken up space next to Cinnabon. With its bright, Halloween-orange sign and an array of colorful baubles in its windows, Spice of Life! stood out in the rundown, often-vacant, mall. A potpourri of curious scents wafted out from the tiny shop, most notably an authentic-smelling pumpkin spice that reminded her of her grandmother's kitchen. Nichole was all too eager to check the store out.

She barely had time to register the rows of spices, tea leaves, and intricately decorated pestles and mortars before she was cordially accosted by a middle-aged woman with silver hair, dressed in a purple, shimmery blouse: "Welcome to Spice of Life!" said the woman, smiling. "I'm Rain, the owner. We just opened this week. We're a seasonal store of a very peculiar stripe."

After her less-than-affable interaction with her yoga classmates, Nichole found the cheery woman welcoming, even if she was only trying to greet a prospective customer. "You wouldn't happen to have any magic potion that could help me lose some weight, do you?" asked Nichole, crossing her hands over her belly.

Rain chuckled. "Well, we don't exactly have 'magic potions,' but I think we might have something to help you lose a few extra pounds, and maybe more. How familiar are you with Pagan witchcraft?"

"I actually dabbled with Wicca in college. I had some roommates who introduced me to it, but it was more of a curiosity at the time than anything else." At this, Rain seemed to grimace, and Nichole quickly corrected herself. "But I've always had a real interest in the practice."

"Follow me." Rain led Nichole down an aisle stocked with candles and glass jars containing a colorful variety of herbs and spices—Adder's Tongue, Brimstone, Monkshood. She stopped and handed Nichole a clear package labeled "Weight Loss and Vitality." Inside were a small booklet, a black candle, some sort of green herb, and a coarse, yellow powder.

"This is all you need to lose that pesky weight. Follow the instructions for this spell—you can even mix it with your tea—and you'll be dropping pounds faster than any exercise or diet fad could do."

"I won't have to hex anyone or convene with Pazuzu for this to work, right?" joked Nichole.

Rain turned serious. "It's all white magick, dear. We don't promote any black spells at Spice of Life!"

"Oh, I'm sorry," said Nichole, embarrassed. "I'll definitely have to give this a try." Rain led her to the cash register and she paid for the kit, then received two punches in her new Spice of Life! Rewards Card.

"Tell your friends!" said Rain, as she handed Nichole an orange bag with a cartoonish witch riding a broom inside a stylish pentagram.

"I will. Thanks!"

The afternoon and evening drifted by uneventfully for Nichole. She prepared a glucose-free pasta dish for her husband, Bill, and son, Aidan, then the family ate quietly, before going their separate ways—Bill to his Yankees and Aidan to his video games.

With both of her men occupied, Nichole went to the basement den, bringing her Spice of Life! kit with her. She was certain Bill would laugh at her new purchase, and besides, she needed privacy to ensure the utmost mental clarity necessary for the ritual. She had retained a little knowledge from her experimental days at Ithaca College.

Nichole took a seat on the sofa and laid out the items necessary for the ritual on the coffee table. Carefully, she followed the spell book's instructions, carving her name into the side of the candle, then lighting it. She burnt the herb in a spoon over the candle, then mixed it with the powder into a hot tea.

She then recited the enclosed spell over her cup:

Sit utero meo erit sepulcrum,
Parere ultra, ego anathema,
Subscribere eius nomen
Ad voluntatem meam

After reading the incantation three times Nichole finally took a sip. She found the concoction surprisingly good.

It was savory, like a strong, pumpkin spice tea, with only a hint of a strange, slightly bitter aftertaste. She finished the tea, fully intending to repeat the process over the coming days.

Nichole then went upstairs, where Bill and Aidan were still occupied by their games. She went to the bathroom and examined herself in the mirror, vainly hoping that she might have undergone an instantaneous, Fairy Godmother-level transformation. She was disappointed when staring back at her was the same shabby woman who couldn't keep her back straight at yoga class.

Weeks passed, and Nichole repeated her tea ritual, stopping in at Spice of Life! to obtain another kit, and then another when she would run out. To her surprise, she began losing weight. She first noticed that her clothes were a better fit, and that the double chin she had grown to hate slowly became less noticeable when she tilted her head. At yoga class, she even found herself keeping up with the other women. Bill took notice and complimented her looks for the first time in years.

After trying every crash diet and spending hundreds on trendy workout videos and books, she was making progress toward her ideal weight—and it was all thanks to a quirky Wiccan shop in the mall!

"You should try it," said Nichole, to Stacy Petcosky, a newer addition to the yoga class. She had told her sole confidant about her secret, after Stacy had complimented her on her ability to sustain her Bridge Pose.

"I don't believe in any of that witch crap," said Stacy, out of breath and sweating profusely, as the women changed together in the locker room. "I'm just looking for a quick and easy way to lose some weight."

"It's not like you put on some pointy black hat and cackle over a bubbling cauldron," said Nichole, slipping on a new, smaller blouse which she had purchased after losing an additional ten pounds. "If you like pumpkin spice or chai, then you'll probably even enjoy it. It's certainly no more hazardous than sucking down teaspoon after teaspoon of apple cider vinegar—trust me, I've done that. And this actually works."

"Maybe," said Stacy.

As the women continued to ready themselves for the day, two of the more supercilious women in class came over to chat with Stacy, at first, completely ignoring Nichole.

"Stacy doll, Jayne and I are headed to the mall to get a present for Link Kristopherson's boy," said Chrissy King.

"We'd love for your company," said Jayne Moore. "Maybe head over to the Lost Dog for an early lunch?"

"Sure, I'd love to," said Stacy. Her husband was the mayor, and she practically knew every wannabe socialite in the Tri-County area because of it; whether she wanted to know these women was another question entirely. "Nichole here was telling me about an interesting new store in the mall that sells some odd herbs, spices, and candles."

Jayne's eyes went wide, while Chrissy smirked.

"Yes, you must see it, Stace!" said Jayne. "It's the tackiest little shop our tacky little mall has ever had."

"There's even a witch on a broom on their logo," said Chrissy, eying Nichole.

Nichole shrank back into her locker as the trio gossiped. She was disappointed when they left and Stacy didn't say goodbye.

Whatever the popular women at her gym thought of the new Wiccan store, Nichole was now a full-fledged Spice of Life! convert. She tried out a variety of other magic kits that the store had to offer. Now that she was quickly approaching her weight loss goal, she wanted more: a better marriage, more money, some semblance of control over her vices.

But she wasn't the only one seemingly benefiting from the Spice of Life! brand. As the weeks went by, she marveled at Stacy's rapid weight loss.

"Stacy, you look fantastic," said Nichole, after class.

"Thanks," said Stacy, who carried herself with a newfound confidence. "I owe it all to you and Spice of Life!"

There were chuckles from the other side of the locker room. Chrissy and Jayne had overheard their conversation.

"You've got to be kidding me," said Chrissy, rolling her eyes.

"About what?" snapped back Nichole, surprised at her own vigor.

"There's no substitute for exercise and a clean diet," said Jayne. "Stacy doll, you're getting duped."

"Then how do you explain all the weight I've lost?" said Stacy. "And Nichole too?"

"I don't know. But it's not some witch's spell," replied Chrissy.

"Stace, you're literally here at the gym exercising every day," said Jayne, laughing.

The conversation then turned to town gossip, birthday parties, and charitable events. None of which involved Nichole.

Nichole burned through one spell kit after another in the following weeks, and she reached her target weight and then some. For the first time in years she noticed the eyes of men lingering on her, including her husband's. Bill was constantly after her, pawing at her all over the house, and they somehow found time to go on dates together.

She was in good spirits one afternoon, when she went to Spice of Life! to replenish her supply and expand her spell catalogue. But as she entered her favorite store her spirit deflated at the sight of Jayne and Chrissy from yoga. They were each holding one of the store's unmistakable orange bags. The two women noticed Nichole and smirked at each other.

"Look who it is," said Jayne. "Nikki the White Witch!"

"Hi," replied Nichole, sheepishly. "I thought you guys didn't believe in this sort of thing."

"Stacy recommended it," said Chrissy. "She's gotten great results using this pumpkin spice weight loss tea. I think she read about it on Goop, actually."

"No, I told Stacy about it; and when I recommended it to her, you guys *actually* laughed," said Nichole, now perturbed.

Jayne rolled her eyes. "Jesus, don't act like you're some fucking trendsetter. It's a store in the *Elmdale Mall.*"

"But you guys made fun of the Wiccan stuff," said Nichole.

"We bought some candles and herbs. Is that okay with you?" said Jayne.

"Yeah, I guess that makes us witches now," said Chrissy. "Jayne, we should probably go to Hot Topic and pick up some emo goth gear."

"Good idea, Chris. Maybe Nichole can come to our slumber party this weekend and we can all watch *The Craft* together," said Jayne.

"And Nichole can play our fat Neve Campbell," said Chrissy. She and Jayne then burst out laughing as they left.

Nichole then drifted further into the store, now practically in tears, when she noticed that Rain, the shop owner, had been listening in on her conversation with her yoga classmates. "Oh, hi Rain. I just..."

"It's okay, dear," said Rain, stepping out from behind a floor display. "You know, there are ways to get back at women like that."

"Sure, I know. I should just ignore them and focus on what I'm working toward. 'Living well is the best revenge,' right?"

"That's a nice notion, but it isn't very satisfying, is it? Follow me. I think I can help."

Nichole followed Rain through a beaded curtain and into the backroom. There was a desk and computer, and a few cubbies for employees' coats and belongings. Rain went to the desk, opened the top drawer, and pulled out an unmarked grey satchel. She turned and handed the bag to Nichole, smiling wickedly.

"If you so choose, this contains a very special hex that you may use. I divined it myself, crafted it to inflict a moderate punishment on a woman, a business partner, who wronged me."

"Really? What happened?" asked Nichole, breathlessly.

"Let's just say that it will make a vain woman suffer a great indignity," said Rain. "While each will suffer differently."

"Isn't that *black magick*?" Nichole was now a full-fledged believer in magick. She was living proof of the power of Wiccan spells, and wholeheartedly believed that Rain's magick was powerful.

"I'm a gray witch," said Rain. "I'm open to all of what magick has to offer. I don't believe there is a right, moral path when casting spells. Only that you should plan on receiving the same energy that you put out into the world."

"Won't something bad happen if I hex someone?"

"Something bad has already happened to you," said Rain. "I've seen and heard it for myself, in fact."

Nichole was weary of dabbling in the dark, but Rain did have a point. Jayne and Chrissy, among others, had been nasty to her for far too long. An eye for an eye. She took the bag from the shopkeeper. "How much is it?"

Rain raised her hands in protest. "No, no. You're my best customer. This one is free."

"I can't thank you enough, Rain," said Nichole. "You've already done so much for me."

The women said their goodbyes and Nichole was off to finish a few errands before she headed home. She wasn't set on using the hex against Chrissy and Jayne, but she told herself she would consider it while weighing her options.

Nichole was early to her next yoga class and had time to chat with Stacy.

"My husband has really come around. We're trying for our second," said Nichole. "I'm hoping for a girl, of course."

"That's really great," said Stacy. "I bet your husband can't keep his hands off you—I know mine has been insatiable lately—you're looking tremendous."

"Thanks for saying so, Stacy!" beamed Nichole.

Just then, Chrissy and Jayne walked into the yoga studio. Nichole couldn't help but overhear their conversation.

"We should try and get pregnant at the same time," said Chrissy.

"We should!" exclaimed Jayne, laughing. "Now I'm *glad* that last month didn't stick. We both have to get pregnant before Halloween, so we can have summer babies!"

Jayne and Chrissy then lay down their mats beside Stacy and Nichole's. They didn't bother greeting Nichole.

"Hey, Stace! You should get pregnant with us too!" said Chrissy.

Stacy grimaced at the thought of it. "One is enough for me, ladies. Nichole here said she and her hubby are trying for number two, though."

Nichole's anxiety welled up in her throat. She hadn't told Stacy about her run-in with Chrissy and Jayne at the mall. She didn't want to bad-mouth Stacy's friends, since she and Stacy were still getting to know each other.

"Oh, we thought you were already preggers, Nikki," said Jayne.

"Nope. And it's 'Nichole.'" She looked toward the door, knowing Wendy would be bounding in any moment.

"Stacy, that Wiccan tea you recommended was no joke," said Chrissy. "I think I've lost five pounds since Tuesday."

Chrissy was already rail-thin. Nichole couldn't imagine it would be all that healthy for her to lose any more weight.

"Yeah, it seems like everyone in the class is using it and getting results," said Stacy. "I'm glad Nichole told me about it."

"That's right," said Chrissy. "Nichole discovered the new witch store in the Elmdale Mall. We should all be grateful for her discovery. I don't know how any of us would've found Spice of Life! across from Cinnabon, and half a mile from this gym."

Stacy busied herself with her phone when Nichole looked to her for support. "Sure thing, glad I could help..." said Nichole, hoping they'd just drop it.

"I started using it the day Stacy mentioned it," said Jayne. "That was weeks ago. I don't know why she shouldn't get the credit."

"I really don't care!" said Nichole, louder than she had wanted to be. The other women who had gradually filtered into the room all stopped and stared.

"Sounds like you don't care," said Chrissy.

Nichole was disappointed when Stacy walked away, as she was obviously trying to avoid being involved.

"The two of you are such *bitches*," said Nichole, softly. "Just leave me the hell alone."

Chrissy and Jayne were taken aback by her sudden frankness, as was the instructor, Wendy, who had overheard the conversation and was clearly incensed by Nichole's choice of words.

"Nichole!" said Wendy, confronting her. "That language is unacceptable in my studio! We come here to relax and meditate."

"It's alright, Wendy. I'm leaving anyway," said Nichole, before storming out of the room in tears.

That night, while Bill and Aidan slept, Nichole went to the basement den with the grey satchel that Rain had given her. She opened the bag and emptied the contents onto the table: a folded piece of paper, which she assumed were the instructions, a square wooden board, chalk, three candles, and a small penknife with a ram's head handle. She read the instructions first:

Draw a pentacle on the oak surface in chalk. Then carve the name of the accursed in the center of the circle. Light the yellow candle and say 'Et flavo lumine eum unitas eat,' then light the black candle and say 'Dico in tenebris Baphometus,' then light the red candle and say 'Offero sacrificium sanguinis pretio!' Now, erase the chalk from the oak surface. Then make an inch-long incision in the left palm, completely covering the name of the accursed in blood.

Nichole wasn't sure that she wanted to cut herself. She was having second thoughts about whether she wanted to put a hex on Jayne and Chrissy; and the spell was certainly darker in its execution than her vitality spell. She considered Rain's rationalization, that they had already harmed her, and her retaliatory magick would only be settling the score. So, Nichole continued with the hex spell, telling herself that she was just resetting the karmic scale.

First, she drew the pentacle from a diagram she found on the internet, then wrote Jayne and Chrissy's names inside the star. Then she lit each candle, carefully reciting each line of the spell. After Nichole had erased the chalk from the oak board, and was preparing herself to cut her own hand, only then did she feel the full weight of what she was about to do.

Once again, she hesitated, knowing that anything could happen when one placed a curse on someone. She had read all the warnings against black magick back in her naive college years—and when thinking back to those innocent days, she dropped the knife to the table. Nichole wasn't going to cut her hand, nor was she going to complete the hex spell. She knew that she would fundamentally alter who she was as a person if she went through with the curse. That she would have lowered herself to their despicable level, just to hurt them. She couldn't stomach the thought of it.

It was Halloween, and Nichole had a special appointment with her obstetrician, Dr. Kominoes.

"Ms. Olsen, the tests and imaging are conclusive," said Dr. Kominoes. "Not only are your ovaries not producing enough estrogen to allow for a successful pregnancy, but the ovarian structures are shriveled."

Nichole was floored by the diagnosis. "Are you saying I'm entering menopause, or something?"

The doctor was genuinely disheartened to break this news to Nichole. He had delivered her son, Aidan, and was also her regular gynecologist. "Premature ovarian failure isn't uncommon in women under forty. I'm sorry, Nichole."

"How did it happen?" She was now weeping gently, coming to terms with the fact that Aidan would never have a sibling and that she would never again experience the joys of caring for a baby of her own.

"Genetics, diet, environment... There are a myriad of reasons why women become infertile. Have you traveled out of the country recently? Had any traumas, car accidents? Have you been exposed to any hazardous chemicals?"

"Not that I can think of..." Nichole's thoughts drifted. She still had a few hours before she would need to get the ice cream to Aidan's Halloween party at school. She felt decent enough to exercise. She had skipped a week of yoga out of embarrassment over her outburst and confrontation with Chrissy and Jayne— she figured it was about time to get back to it. It would certainly distract her from her current health issue...

"Ms. Olsen?" said Dr. Kominoes. "Nichole?"

"I'm sorry. Yes, a follow-up appointment for another ultrasound after Thanksgiving sounds fine."

"There's always the possibility that hormone therapy might revitalize your ovaries," said Dr. Kominoes. "But it's very expensive, and we'd have to pinpoint the cause of your premature ovarian failure."

Nichole scheduled the follow-up appointment with the clinic's secretary, and not twenty minutes later she was walking through the door of the yoga studio at Sure-Fit. Her tardiness drew a few stares, especially since her classmates hadn't seen her since she had walked out. The class was uneventful—Jayne was absent, to Nichole's relief—and Wendy even complimented her form on her Downward-Facing Dog Pose.

After class, Stacy struck up a conversation with Nichole. "Hey Nic, I just want to say I'm sorry for dipping out when Jayne and Chrissy were giving you a hard time."

"It's just so childish," said Nichole. "I'll never understand women like them."

"You mean bullies?" said Stacy. "Did you notice how Chrissy was the first girl out of here after class?"

Nichole nodded. "She doesn't know what to do without Jayne around."

"Speaking of Jayne..." Stacy looked around to make sure no one could overhear. "I heard from a mutual friend that she's having major health problems."

"Really?"

"Yeah, I'm not sure about the details, but she's scheduled for an emergency hysterectomy."

"Oh, wow," said Nichole, thinking of her own health issues. "I'm actually having problems myself. The doc seems to think my ovaries have shut down."

Stacy hugged Nichole. "I'm really sorry to hear that. A few other girls have been having fertility problems."

"Girls in class?"

Stacy nodded. "Last class, that redhead Lynn, who's usually up in the front, was talking about some sort of ovarian failure. Another girl has some bad cysts…"

"Premature ovarian failure?" asked Nichole, her thoughts now racing.

"Yeah, that sounds right," said Stacy. "All these fertility issues, just in this class alone. It's almost like an epidemic."

"Or a curse," said Nichole.

"Yeah…" said Stacy, now deep in thought. "What would we all have in common?"

Nichole thought of all the possible connections between herself and her classmates. Beyond the yoga studio, and the fact that they were all young, fit women, there was really nothing else to tie them together, nothing but a small store in the mall.

"Spice of Life!" said Nichole, grimly. "How about we get changed and go over to the store. We can get a few of the kits for my doctor to test."

"Sounds like a plan," said Stacy. "It's not like those magick kits were FDA approved."

When Nichole and Stacy entered the Elmdale Mall they were shocked to find an empty storefront where Spice of Life! had been. Nichole pushed her face against the glass to try and see if there was any stock left in the store, but it was completely barren; even the orange sign had been taken down. A teenage girl dressed up like a zombie, behind the counter at the Cinnabon, told them that the store had closed shop just the day before.

"It's a seasonal place," said the zombie cashier. "Halloween and witches and all that. She did great business, though. It was probably the busiest store in the mall over the past couple of weeks. I'm surprised she didn't stay open for Halloween."

"Samhain is a holiday for Wiccans," said Nichole. "Do you know how we might get ahold of the owner of Spice of Life!?

The zombie shrugged. "I'd go to the mall offices and ask them. They should know her contact info."

"Thanks!"

Stacy and Nichole did go to the mall offices and speak with a manager-type. But he couldn't give them much information about Rain or her store, besides for a phone number that ended up being out of service.

When more of Nichole's classmates found themselves with fertility problems in the following weeks, it quickly became evident to everyone involved that there was more than a tenuous link between Spice of Life!'s magick kits and their reproductive issues. A few of the women were still in possession of unused kits, and Nichole was able to bring those to Dr. Kominoes for testing.

"Well, did you hear back from your doc?" asked Chrissy. She, Jayne, Stacy and half of the class were already standing in a semi-circle around Nichole's locker as soon she arrived that morning.

"Yes. It's bad," said Nichole, anxious about how everyone would take the news.

"Get on with it, please," said Lynn.

"It wasn't just the Weight Loss and Vitality kit that was contaminated," stated Nichole. "The lab at Memorial Hospital found a specific chemical that can cause ovarian failure and various fertility issues in all of the samples from the kits—it's a really long chemical name that I can't pronounce, but I wrote it down for everyone." She handed out copies of the lab report with a note from Dr. Kominoes to all present.

"This says it's 'a chemical most commonly found in pesticides,'" said Jayne. "*Why the hell* was that mixed in with our pumpkin spice chai?"

"We were poisoned by that witch!" shouted Chrissy.

"I'm never going to have a child because I was poisoned by a witch from the mall?" said Lynn, before she began hyperventilating.

The mob crowded in around Nichole. Some women cried and hugged each other, some raged and screamed about the injustice that had been done to them.

"It's Nichole's fault!" cried Jayne, as mascara trickled down her sobbing face. "She told everyone about that stupid store and pushed that poison on all of us!"

"Don't, Jayne!" yelled Stacy, but she was drowned out by the mob who were cursing Nichole along with the witch Rain.

They pawed and grabbed at Nichole as she rushed out of the locker room. She didn't make it out unscathed; her exercise shirt was in tatters, and she lost a small chunk of hair as she was forced to push her way through the melee. She knew she could never show her face again at Sure-Fit, or in any yoga studio in the Tri-County area.

When she got home she went right down to her basement den. She moved with purpose as she re-drew the pentacle on the wooden board and carved an additional name below Chrissy and Jayne's: Rain. Nichole lit each candle and recited each line of the spell with a newfound malice—and this time she didn't hesitate when it was time to bleed her hand with the small, ornate knife. She smeared her palm on the oaken board as she cursed her enemies, making sure each letter of each name was covered in her blood.

NEIGHBORHOOD FLESH EATERS

As they did most evenings, twin brothers Zack and Sean Grady entered their home filthy from an afternoon's adventure, running their mouths about hijinks they had taken part in around their working-class neighborhood on the northside of Lestershire. They likely would have stayed out past dark were it not for their mother, Faye, who had finally coaxed them inside, threatening that she would confiscate their Xbox if they didn't come in for dinner. When they finally entered their modest home, their father, Ron, was already at the table, irritated and tired, as he usually was after a day managing the EZ-Fill Gas and Gulp on Memorial Drive.

"Wash your hands and come sit down," said Ron, sternly.

"We saw a raccoon by Mr. Farrell's house," said Zack, segue be damned.

Sean piped in; he had to follow up his brother with some additional, niftier detail. "Yeah, and it was carrying a big bone."

Ed took a large spoonful of Hamburger Helper from the glass dish. "Stay away from raccoons—you'll get rabies. And stay away from Mr. Farrell's house too. The man's been through enough these last few months. Last thing he needs is two kids running around his property, chasing rodents."

Mr. Farrell—Jay Farrell as he was known to the adults on Zoa Ave.—lived alone in the house next door, though he wasn't a bachelor by choice. The middle-aged man had once had a beloved wife and daughter, both of whom had drowned during a camping trip to the Catskills. There had been no funeral service nor public viewing, and the boys had immediately picked up on Mr. Farrell's changed temperament in the ensuing months—no more was he the jovial neighbor, the every-dad, father to their school pal Alexis.

"We're not bothering him. He's never out during the day anyway," said Zack. He looked at his brother and grinned. "Sean and I think maybe he's turned into a vampire."

Faye finished dishing out the boys' food and sat down and enjoyed the warm meal she had prepared for her family.

"He's not a vampire," she said, shaking her head. "He works nights at the hospital. Jeez, guys, I work nights at the laundromat. Does that make me a vampire too?"

The boys laughed at their mother. "Maybe," said Sean, who then crossed his fingers in Faye's direction because a holy crucifix wasn't at hand.

"Back to the raccoon," said Ron. "I was talking to Rex Martin and he told me his dog Skeet is missing, as are a bunch of other cats and dogs on the block. Now I've seen you boys mutilate bugs, burn ants with magnifying glasses, and dress Mrs. Ellsic's dog up in lady's clothes—all sorts of nonsense—so I hope you know that if you're at all involved in the disappearance of any of these missing animals, you're in for a world of hurt."

The two brothers said they had nothing to do with any missing animals, then finished their meals. After being excused from the table, they went to their bedroom and played video games for hours. At 9:30 p.m., Faye told them to go to sleep, but Sean and Zack merely turned off their bedroom light and switched to portable consoles to continue their gameplay.

They were in the middle of a heated battle in their favorite fighting game when the window facing Mr. Farrell's house was illuminated by an incoming vehicle.

"Drac is back," said Zack, grinning. He went to the window and peeked through the blind. "Hold up—it's not Mr. Farrell. It's some delivery truck."

"It's almost midnight," said Sean, whose eyes had grown blurry after nearly four hours of uninterrupted gameplay. He stood next to his brother and peeped out the window. The night was black save for the glow of fluorescent light coming from Mr. Farrell's garage. It illuminated the truck, which bore a "Lupo's Refrigeration Company" logo on its side. They watched in silence as a burly man loaded two large crates from the back of the truck and into Mr. Farrell's garage. They were taller than the man.

"What do you think is in the crates?" asked Sean.

Zack shrugged. "I don't know. Maybe it's a couple caskets from Romania or Transylvania or something."

Mr. Farrell then came into view. He signed some paper and the burly man got into his truck and backed out of the driveway. Zack and Sean watched as Mr. Farrell took a crowbar and began to pry one of the crates open. The boys waited with an anticipatory glee to see what was inside. But their hopes of witnessing any monster movie magic were dashed when Mr. Farrell stopped what he was doing and pressed a button on the wall, closing the garage door and concealing his deeds.

"Shit!" said Zack.

"We didn't get to see the caskets," whined Sean.

"There are no caskets, dweeb. You saw the truck—it's some new refrigerators. You've seen Mr. Farrell in the day; he's not a vampire. I was just messing around. He's just been acting a little weird since Mrs. Farrell and Alexis died."

"I miss Alexis. She was cool," said Sean.

"Yeah," replied Zack, who had hung out at the park with Mr. Farrell's daughter just days before her death.

The brothers went back to their video games. Another hour had passed when Sean noticed someone across the street. Only people looking for trouble were out that late.

"Zack, look."

Walking up the sidewalk, carrying a large net, was Mr. Farrell.

"Weeeeeird," said Zack. They were again drawn to the window, focusing on the strange nocturnal exploits of their woeful neighbor. He seemed to be tracking something, because he crouched beside a bush and slowly inched toward an unseen object in the dark. They both startled when Mr. Farrell lunged into the shrubbery and out of sight.

"What the hell!" said Zack. He moved to the other window to try and get a better look, but Mr. Farrell had disappeared into the night.

"Mom, I think Mr. Farrell is the one capturing cats and dogs at night," said Zack the next morning over a bowl of Count Chocula.

Faye rolled her eyes at her dimwitted son. "Right. And Dr. Godbere found worms in someone's teeth," she said, referencing another one of her son's far-fetched stories.

"I'm serious, Mom. Sean, tell her."

"He had a net and was walking around and acting weird," said Sean.

"Leave that poor man alone. Maybe he was out catching moths or something."

"At one in the morning?" said Zack.

Faye leered at her boys. "What were the two of you doing up at 1 a.m.?"

"I couldn't sleep," said Zack.

"Me neither," Sean added.

Faye smirked; they were terrible liars. "Who knows what you saw. All I know is that Mr. Farrell is a good man who doesn't deserve a couple kids cooking up strange stories about him."

The boys stopped talking about Mr. Farrell in front of their mother, but it didn't stop them from blabbing about their weird neighbor during lunch at school, or on the bus ride home, or as they played video games that night in their room. Ron and Faye had gone out—Ron to bowl with his drinking buddies and Faye to her shift at the laundromat—so the boys were home alone to make trouble as they wish, and they wanted to find out whether Mr. Farrell was trapping animals and keeping them in his new refrigerators.

They were discussing the logistics of breaking and entering when their bedroom window was again lit up by a vehicle backing down Mr. Farrell's driveway. They sprung from their beds to see who it was this time.

"Holy shit," said Zack. "It's a hearse, Sean."

The sight of a vehicle so associated with morbidity and the macabre in their neighbor's driveway at night unnerved the brothers, as it was surely out of the ordinary. The only places you ever saw a hearse was at a funeral home or at the cemetery.

"Do you think Mr. Farrell died?" asked Sean.

"No. There he is right there," said Zack.

Mr. Farrell appeared in the driveway and approached the vehicle. The driver stepped out and the boys recognized him as Mr. Coleman, the director of Coleman Funeral Home.

Mr. Coleman opened the rear door of the hearse and the boys watched in silence as the funeral director and Mr. Farrell struggled to lift a large, black bag from the back. The men quickly hoisted the cumbersome object and carried it into the garage.

"What was that in the bag?" asked Sean.

"A fucking body from the funeral home, I'm pretty sure," said Zack.

Sean's eyes widened. "What do you mean? Why would they bring a body *into* someone's house?"

Zack shook his head.

Mr. Coleman exited Mr. Farrell's house and got back in the hearse. The car wasn't gone five minutes before the brothers heard a loud buzzing coming from Mr. Farrell's house. The man's basement light was on, though his thick black curtains blocked any chance of peeking in through the windows.

"Sounds like a table saw," said Zack. The piercing, grinding noise was unmistakable. The sawing went on for hours, as if Mr. Farrell was in the middle of a major home improvement project.

When Faye returned home that night, Zack called his mom into their room and pointed out the loud buzzing still emanating from next door.

"Will you drop this thing with Mr. Farrell, please? It's not healthy."

"What's he doing sawing all night?" said Sean, who was reading a comic book on his bed.

"It's none of your business. Maybe he's fixing something. Maybe he's building model airplanes like your dad used to."

"Maybe he's sawing up bodies to eat," said Zack.

Faye scowled at him. "No more comic books or video games tonight," she said, then left the room.

"Your think Mr. Farrell is a cannibal?" asked Sean.

Zack stared out the window, at Mr. Farrell's ordinary two-story home, wondering what debauched deeds had been done there. "The big refrigerators, the hearse and body bag, him walking around the other night with that net. Something is up, and we're going to find out what."

"How?"

"Tomorrow night, when Mom and Dad are at work, we're breaking into Mr. Farrell's house!"

Thursday nights, both Ron and Faye worked late. Most weeks, this meant that Zack and Sean would have full reign over the house and would feast on Little Debbie snack cakes and play Xbox on the big living room TV that Ron usually monopolized. But this night was different; the boys had a mission. They were going to find out whether their neighbor was a psychotic flesh eater.

When Mr. Farrell left that night, presumably for work, the brothers didn't waste any time beginning their investigation.

"Okay, he's gone," said Zack, grabbing a flashlight from a kitchen drawer. "Let's go."

Sean nervously followed his brother out the back door and into the unseasonably warm, early autumn night. "How do you know he won't be right back?"

"He works nights, like Mom said. It's night, dude."

Zack crept around the Farrell property, Sean right behind him, looking for a way inside. But their neighbor kept a secure home and every door and window on the first floor was locked tight.

"I guess we're shit out of luck, unless I bust a window," said Zack.

"Look," said Sean. He pointed to a window on the second floor that was open just a crack, below which was a wooden trellis.

"Good idea," said Zack, grinning.

He surveyed the neighborhood, making sure no one was watching them either from the street or from a window, then climbed up the trellis. When he reached the top, he pushed the window open further and climbed inside, Sean right behind him.

"This is Alexis' old room," said Zack. The room looked as if Mr. Farrell's deceased daughter might come home any minute. The bed was dressed in a shiny, pink comforter and pillow set. On the walls were posters of her favorite pop acts and pictures of Alexis and her friends at various places around Lestershire.

"Why does he still have her room set up?" asked Sean, looking at the girly knick-knacks that decorated her desk.

"I don't know. Maybe he didn't feel like taking it down," said Zack, who felt guilty for a moment that he was invading the home of a man who had tragically lost his daughter and wife. "Let's just go to the basement."

Zack and Sean walked through the dark home, then downstairs to the kitchen. It was an older house, built during the early 20th century for the employees of the Lester Shoe and Boot Co., and with each step they took came creaks and groans from the old wood, almost as if the house was telling them: "You shouldn't be here."

When Zack unlatched then opened the basement door, he gagged. "Nasty!" They were buffeted by the strong stench of decay, as if they had just opened an overflowing garbage can in the dead of summer.

"It smells like the meat section at Akel's Market," said Sean, before covering his face with his T-shirt.

Zack flipped the light switch and they slowly descended the aged stairs.

"Holy shit, there are animal parts everywhere," said Zack, looking at the mess that lay before them. A large table was set in the center of the room, on which lay a sickening pile of bones, tufts of fur, and various appendages and parts that neither of them were able to identify.

"Zack, I want to leave," said Sean, whose sense of adventure had been eclipsed by an overwhelming dread.

"Look, they aren't refrigerators, they're some sort of freezer," said Zack, ignoring his brother's plea. "We need to find out what's inside." He motioned toward the two large freezer closets resting side-by-side against a wall. He crept toward them, but Sean remained by the table. Zack's heart thumped against his rib cage as he approached the freezers, still curious but also terrified that his cannibal theory may prove correct. Slowly, he opened the first door, and was perplexed to find it stuffed with large trash bags.

"What do you think's in these?" asked Zack, untwisting the top of the bag.

Sean shook his head. "I don't know. Hungry Man dinners?" he said, nervously.

Zack waited no further to uncover Mr. Farrell's deeds. He pulled the bag open, revealing a blue, veiny human leg!

"Holy shit!" shouted Zack.

"Zack, is that real?"

"I think so," said Zack, with a newfound uneasiness. Gone was the thrilling, Hardy Boys-level anticipation he'd had prior to the excursion. Now he was forced to face the chilling reality, and it made him sick to his stomach knowing that his neighbor, Jay Farrell, was a cannibal. "Get over here and open some of the other bags."

Sean, wanting to get the reveal over with so that he and Zack could return to the safety of their bedroom, joined his brother in the open freezer. There wasn't room inside for them both to work, so he removed a bag from the chill interior. Zack watched, his teeth now chattering, as his brother opened the second bag. They both shrieked at its contents. Staring back at them was a human head.

Sean dropped the bag and the head fell out and rolled across the cement floor. It appeared to have belonged to an elderly woman. The hair was long and grey, and the face still had its heavy, funerary makeup. Sean finally reached his breaking point. He began puking out his guts into the open trash bag.

"The guy's a cannibal..." stated Zack, still searching through bags in the freezer while his brother attempted to gather his wits about him.

"We gotta call the cops!" said Sean, between dry-heaves.

"Dude, wait," said Zack, closing the freezer behind him. "What's in the *other* freezer?"

"The police can deal with it. Let's just go," whined Sean, backing away from the tall, stainless steel box.

But there was no turning back for Zack. Though he was still nauseous and overwhelmed by the gravity of his discoveries so far that night, he had to know what horrors lay inside the second freezer. He grabbed the handle and began to open the door...

"Jesus Christ!" Zack and Sean both screamed as two ghastly figures emerged from the cold, lunging toward them.

The ghouls clawed and snarled at them as the brothers tried to tear themselves away. Their skin was pale-blue, and their eyes were devoid of life. They were like wolves after the slaughter, while the boys pushed and kicked back to keep them at bay. The larger of the pair dug her nails into Zack's arm, breaking skin, before he put some distance between himself and his attacker.

"It's Mrs. Farrell and Alexis!" shouted Sean, who had managed to take cover behind Mr. Farrell's work table. "I think they're zombies!"

"Duh!" said Zack, as he joined his brother behind the table.

They were able to avoid the women by running around the table and the nearby workbench, always keeping a barrier between themselves and their deceased neighbors.

"What are we supposed to do?" shouted Sean. "I don't think we can run upstairs without them grabbing us."

"We'll have to figure something out," said Zack, as he dodged behind Mr. Farrell's tool chest, narrowly avoiding Alexis' grasp—Alexis Farrell, who had been a cherubic, raven-haired beauty, and the girl whom Zack had had a secret crush on for years.

Zack and Sean were able to force a stalemate with the ghouls, for some time, as the women would predictably lunge across the table while the boys slipped behind the nearby workbench, and vice versa.

Zack looked to the open freezer and began to formulate a plan. "I'm gonna close myself in the freezer with the body parts. They'll rush at the door, so you'll have to then distract them away from it, so I can get out."

"No! Why?" said Sean. His face was red, and he was sweating profusely from his exertion, and the adrenaline dump brought on by his sustained state of panic.

"If I get a few legs or arms out, I might be able to distract them long enough for us to run upstairs."

"That won't work…" Sean didn't get to finish his thought, as Zack was already running toward the freezer.

Just as he said he would, he closed himself in the freezer, while Mrs. Farrell and Alexis pounded at the door trying to get at him, both incapable of operating a basic latch handle. Sean first looked to the stairs, knowing that it was the perfect chance to get away. But it was only a fleeting thought; he knew he couldn't abandon his brother.

Sean began pounding on the table with a hammer and yelling at the zombies, but it did nothing to distract them from their target within the freezer. Next, he tried throwing things at them, but they still wouldn't move. He was terrified at the thought of it, but he knew what he had to do.

"Hey, come eat me, Mrs. Farrell!" Sean ran toward the zombies and they instantly gave chase. Alexis soon had a hold of his shirt, and he couldn't slip out of it, running as the fabric stretched from his body to her long, black fingernails. Mrs. Farrell caught up, lunging at him, causing all three to tumble to the floor together.

"No!" screamed Sean, realizing his predicament, as he tried to scramble away but was stuck under the weight of Mrs. Farrell. He held Alexis' head back as she snapped her teeth inches from his face and yelped when

Mrs. Farrell dug her nails into his side as she rearranged herself to get at him.

"Get off my brother!" screamed Zack as he flew from the foggy, frozen container. He carried a leg with him and swung it at Mrs. Farrell, knocking her to her side. Sean's trapped leg was freed, allowing him to kick Alexis and roll away.

Zack then clobbered Alexis with the appendage as she was about to retake Sean. Sean was able to get up, and as he did he narrowly avoided Mrs. Farrell. She chased him behind the workbench and then around the table, while Zack backed toward the freezer, calling to Alexis.

"Lexi, I just wanna tell you that I think you're the hottest girl in school, and I wanna take you out to dinner..." Zack didn't get to finish his confession, as Alexis was coming at him. He bashed her with the leg, then pushed her into the freezer with the bagged body parts while she was dazed, successfully shutting the door before she could get to her feet.

Zack turned around. Seeing that Mrs. Farrell was still distracted by his brother, he grabbed the trash bag from the floor, briefly stumbling over the elderly woman's head, and crept toward Mrs. Farrell. When he was close enough, he pulled the large, heavy duty bag over the woman's head, down to her waist. She flailed as Zack tried to pin her arms to her sides and guide her toward the other, unoccupied freezer.

"Sean, help me!"

Sean quickly realized what Zack was up to and ran around to shoulder tackle the writhing zombie. They pushed and pulled the woman across the room and into the freezer, briefly pinning Zack against the back of the unit. Sean pulled Zack out by both of his arms and together they shut the door on Mrs. Farrell.

"Okay, now we can go," said Zack, as he was bent over, trying to catch his breath.

The boys hurried up the basement steps and opened the door to the Farrell's dimly lit kitchen, both ecstatic to have an exit in sight.

"Let's get home and call Dad," said Zack, as the pair glided toward the back door.

But before Zack could reach for the handle, the door opened. Mr. Farrell was startled to see the boys in his kitchen and stepped back. Sean noticed that he was carrying a blue cooler with 'Property of Memorial Hospital' stenciled to its side.

"What are you boys doing in here?" asked Mr. Farrell, stepping inside as the boys took a step back. He flipped on the light and immediately noticed that the basement door was ajar.

"Uh, we were in Alexis' room," said Zack, his voice trembling. "We were looking for her diary."

"You were in the basement," said Mr. Farrell.

Sean began to whimper, knowing that they were caught in the act.

"Yeah..." said Zack, considering whether they had any other options for a quick exit.

"You saw them?" asked Mr. Farrell.

Both boys nodded.

"You probably think I killed them or something," said Mr. Farrell. "But I've been trying to keep them alive."

"What do you mean?" asked Zack. "They're dead."

"Yes, I know. I'm trying to keep them stable until I can figure out who to take them to," said Mr. Farrell. "There's gotta be someone out there who'll know how to cure them."

"What's with all the dead animals and the cut-up..." said Sean.

"The corpse? I had the girls trapped in the basement. But it was like they were dying. I needed to feed them *something*," said Mr. Farrell. "I tried different raw meats, roadkill—but they needed something fresher. I love animals, but I love my family more."

"The neighborhood pets?" asked Zack.

"Yes, it seemed like the animals would sustain them, but it got harder catching them," said Mr. Farrell. "So, I resorted to stealing limbs and organs from the hospital. But there aren't all that many limbs and organs lying around hospitals, so I acquired the corpse."

"We saw Mr. Coleman's hearse..." said Zack.

"Yes. I know it's wrong. It is wrong. But the lady was going to be cremated anyway," said Mr. Farrell. He dropped the cooler to the kitchen counter.

"Did they get bit by zombies when you were camping?" asked Sean, who had been quietly listening.

"No, they really did drown," said Mr. Farrell. "They were taken to the morgue, examined. I work for the medical examiner—in the morgue. I was walking the halls of the sub-basement right after it happened. I couldn't go home, I couldn't leave them..."

"They came back to life?" asked Zack, dry-mouthed and in awe of Mr. Farrell's story.

"No. I brought them back to life," said Mr. Farrell. "I was lost, wandering the halls late at night, when an older man in a suit stopped me. He knew exactly what had happened and he had answers. He offered me a way to bring them back, and I took it.

"Mr. Coleman helped me. We faked all the paperwork. I got them home and they seemed to be regaining consciousness. I thought they were going to be the same when they came to, but they weren't. It was like they got stuck somewhere between life and death..."

"Do you think they can be un-, um, zombified?" asked Zack.

"I don't know," said Mr. Farrell, his eyes now vacant, as if his thoughts were somewhere else. "I regret bringing them back now. I shouldn't have made that deal..."

"Mr. Farrell, we can help!" said Zack. "We can trap squirrels and cats. We're practically experts."

"Squirrels and cats are too small. They need bigger game, so they don't fade," said Mr. Farrell, eying Sean.

"I promise we won't tell anyone," said Sean, feeling the heavy gaze of the older man upon him.

"Yeah, you can trust us," said Zack, sweating through his T-shirt. "Alexis was one of our best friends. We'd do anything to get her back to normal."

"Like I said, they need bigger, fresher things to sustain them," said Mr. Farrell, grasping each boy by the shoulder and leading them toward the basement door...

VISITING HOURS

"I'm sorry, but the cemetery is closed for the winter. Visiting hours will resume in the spring," said John Moore, caretaker of the Sunshire Hill Cemetery.

A woman who looked to be in her mid-fifties stood at the gate. She was taken aback that she wouldn't be able to visit her son, as she had done daily, since his death two months prior.

"What do you mean? I can't visit my son's grave?"

John approached the gate; he'd been clearing old flower containers and fallen American flags, readying the graveyard for a long northern winter. He stood opposite the grieving woman, with the black, iron gate between them. He had seen her once before, visiting the Kelly grave when it was still fresh. "I can only get out here once a week during the winter. Soon the snow and ice will be covering the paths, and most days it'll be unsafe for visitors."

"I don't care if there's snow or ice," said Mrs. Kelly. "The paths are clear now. I want to visit my son."

"It doesn't matter what you want, ma'am," said John. "It's the cemetery board's policy. Our insurance won't cover an accident that might occur on a slick path during the winter season."

Mrs. Kelly was irate. "I paid five thousand dollars for a plot for my son, and now I want to visit him. Seems like that should give me the right to visit here any damn time I want."

John was 63, still working full-time, while Sunshire was merely a side gig for him. He had dealt with every type of person in his years working as an electrician for a local utility company and no longer had much patience for the hardheaded folks who believed that they were the exception to the rule. "The visitation hours, including the seasonal changes, were made clear in the contract that you signed to acquire the plot, ma'am. If you don't like how things are run here, you can have your son reburied elsewhere." With that John turned and walked away.

Mrs. Kelly was stunned. She had merely wanted to visit her son's grave and was bristled by the caretaker's lack of respect for her and her boy. "You nasty man. Have you no empathy?!" But John kept walking, not even flinching when she had cried out.

Mrs. Kelly wept at the gate, angrily vowing to the caretaker that she would be let into the cemetery to see her son before the first snowfall.

John braced for the blowback regarding his dealings with Mrs. Kelly. Surely, she would get into contact with one of Sunshire's board members, and he would be harangued for telling the shrewish woman that she could take her business elsewhere. But then a full week passed, and no call came.

However, the following Sunday, when he went back to the cemetery for the first time since his argument with Mrs. Kelly, he found a cornstalk effigy on the front gate. It was shaped like a man, nearly three-feet tall, with arms outspread and hands secured to the gate as if it were being crucified.

John tossed the cornstalk man aside and checked the gate lock for tampering. After unlocking the gate and walking the cemetery grounds, he found nothing amiss and went about his chores. He considered it a message from Mrs. Kelly, though he had no idea what it meant.

Over the course of the day his thoughts often returned to the effigy—what purpose it served, whether it was some sort of threat that needed deciphering. He was puzzled by it, so much so that the next morning he went out of his way to drive past the cemetery on his way to work.

It was just after dawn, and as he drove up the partially paved road to Sunshire Hill Cemetery, he never would have guessed that his questions concerning the cornstalk man would soon be answered, and horrifically so. He first spotted Mrs. Kelly's black sedan, and hoped he'd catch her in the act of trespassing. When he turned, and his truck lights shone in the general direction of the cemetery proper, he saw Mrs. Kelly standing before the closed gate, with a new effigy before her. This cornstalk man appeared in the same position as the effigy from the day before. John was about to drive up and tear the dummy down, when he saw someone approaching from the other side of the gate.

He stopped the car some distance from the cemetery entrance and watched as a man slowly approached and met Mrs. Kelly at the gate. At first, John was confused by the scene, though he sensed that it was somehow unnatural—that the man on the other side of the gate rightfully belonged there. John was a sensible person and had never given any thought to the supernatural or occult, but as he watched this surreal scene unfold, he considered whether Mrs. Kelly might be using the cornstalk effigy to summon the man. Whether it was her deceased son or some other ghoul,

John wasn't willing to stick around and find out. Mrs. Kelly had never once turned to address John's approaching vehicle, so when he turned and drove off, he believed that she had been unaware of his intrusion.

John left Sunshire Hill and went to work, unsuccessfully trying to put aside his morning's vision. It was a long day of power line maintenance for him and his utility crew, and all he could do was obsess over Mrs. Kelly's witchery. The day's discussion revolved around football and word of the season's first snowfall, all the while John was considering who he should contact about what he had seen. The police would think he was a madman. The Sunshire board of directors would likely fire him. Would his priest believe him? He wondered whether it was better to just stay away from Sunshire Hill altogether.

By the time John returned home that evening he was physically and mentally fatigued. His anxiety was giving him bad indigestion; it felt like someone was throttling his esophagus. He lived alone and looked forward to the silence and comfort of his abode. However, when he pulled into his driveway he spied something on his front door which gave him pause. He got out of his truck and went up the path to get a better look, and it didn't take him long to realize what hung on his door. It was a cornstalk effigy, the same height and style as the ones he'd seen on the gate at Sunshire.

The only major, and rightfully distressing, difference was that this cornstalk man was crucified upside down! John got close enough to see the thick nails driven into his door. He assumed that this meant he would soon get an otherworldly visitor. He was terrified by the thought of some ghoul knocking on his door that evening. John turned abruptly and returned to his pickup. He could only think of one course of action.

As John raced to the cemetery his arms and legs felt heavy; it was difficult for him to move his foot from the gas to the brake. He truly believed a supernatural force was at play, something sinister, slowly infiltrating his body. He had to lift his leg to move his foot onto the break, to avoid crashing into the stone wall that surrounded Sunshire.

He staggered out of his truck and opened the heavy, black gate, avoiding contact with the same cornstalk effigy that he had seen that morning. He continued to the gravesite of Mrs. Kelly's son, Christopher Kelly, who had passed away in his thirties. He saw that the grave was still dirt-clad and tightly packed from the burial, and there was no evidence that it had been disturbed. However, the untouched grave brought him no relief.

John returned to the cemetery gate to stand watch, now sweating profusely, unsure of whether the leaden weight would ever be lifted from his person. He had an ax and a shotgun in his truck and considered grabbing them to defend himself. He had been prepared to confront anything or anyone that might arise that evening and menace him, long before they arrived at his home—but that was before he had felt the indomitable tightness in his chest, before he had trouble seeing straight from a swelling migraine that threatened to topple him.

It felt inevitable when Mrs. Kelly arrived in her black sedan. She stopped outside the gate and exited the vehicle. John felt her icy presence infiltrating his body, running down his spine, as soon as she stepped out onto the road. She walked past him without comment, without so much as a glance in his direction. He watched Mrs. Kelly go to the grave of her son and stand vigil for an hour. John didn't move, waiting patiently for the pain in his head to subside, or for her to raise the dead.

But nothing fantastic occurred, and Mrs. Kelly returned to her car, while John's spell of suffering ebbed. The first snow of the season then began falling and John got back into his truck, now completely in control of all his faculties. When he arrived back home, he was greatly relieved to find no trace of the cornstalk effigy on his front door.

From that day on, he was much kinder, and accommodating, regarding Mrs. Kelly's visitations, even going so far as to salt and shovel her a path directly to her son's grave when it snowed.

A HAMMOCK CAMPING HOW-TO

The Peekamoose swimming hole was far too crowded that evening for Anthony Pufky to get quality footage for his YouTube channel, Lost in the Catskills. His subscribers had come to expect remote locations that they could visit themselves and still experience a sense of adventure and discovery. He was also becoming known for his tips on finding the best hiking, camping, and swimming spots, places not everyone and their brother had already tagged on Instagram.

Not wanting to waste a long trip from his home in New Paltz, and having recently acquired a new, lightweight camping hammock from a sponsor, Anthony decided on an impromptu overnight in the nearby Sundown Wild Forest. He retrieved his overnight bag, leaving his car at the trailhead for the Blue Hole, and headed north into the forest, following Bear Hole Brook.

It was approaching sunset, so Anthony knew he had to hurry if he wanted to have enough light to set up his hammock and also film the process. He followed the brook for nearly two miles before he spied a clearing, which let additional light into the darkening forest. There he found two hearty pines at just the right distance apart to secure his hammock.

Anthony wasted no time setting up his sleeping area, recording the complicated process, since it was more of a suspended one-man *tent* than what one might picture when thinking of a regular hammock.

"It's an artform, really. You must find just the right tension, so you don't immediately sink to the ground. If it's too taught, you might just flip over when you get in," said Anthony, speaking to his small HD handheld camera. "I prefer to be about four feet off the ground when I'm inside, but I'm also taller than most people."

Anthony filmed the sparse forest surrounding his green hammock. He then turned and showed the brook, which lay partially obscured by trees and undergrowth. "Always remember, your campsite needs to be at least 150 feet from water. I'm just far enough that I can still hear the brook, at a slightly higher elevation, which should help keep the mosquitos at bay. There's a nice breeze every so often that comes from the clearing to the west, although it brings with it an earthy, skunky scent that isn't very pleasant."

Anthony turned back to get a closeup of the netting of the hammock. "This should keep most insects out," he said. "It's basically a cocoon. There'll be no openings once I'm zipped up inside, and I think it'll be really comfortable with this sleeping pad that I brought."

After Anthony had eaten some dried food, drank a couple bottles of water and relieved himself, he secured himself in his hammock. He turned his camera on inside his canvas shelter, flipping on the night vision feature. "Here's my view from inside. As you can see, I have an excellent field of vision. I can even see my bag in the tree nearby, which I secured in case of opossums, raccoons, and such... Yes, there are black bears, but I'm not overly worried about them. I do have a can of bear spray in here, a flashlight in case I need to pee, and a bottle of water, because I think I'm in for a warm, muggy night." Anthony showed his items to the camera before signing off.

Not long after Anthony had fallen asleep, he was awoken by the sound of rummaging on the forest floor. It was a soulless dark that night, but he had become accustomed to that feeling of isolation from his numerous solo trips that summer. He found his camera and turned it on, so he could look out and not disturb whatever was rooting around and grumbling within feet of the hammock.

Skunks. He sighed quietly. They were big boys, too. He watched a pair fight over a root or stick just to his right, through the night vision of his camera. He grew anxious when a few passed under him, or paused near him, as he knew he was an easy target, and skunks usually needed little cause to spray a fellow forest dweller. Anthony tried not to think about the ramifications if a few of them decided to start spraying him as he hung in the air.

He put the camera away and began to settle back into his place in the forest while he listened to the skunks rummage for grubs, hiss, and occasionally screech at each other, and eventually he fell back to sleep.

It was the middle of the night, and Anthony's shirt was soaked in sweat the next time he awoke. At first, he was confused where he was, as he had heard an approaching vehicle, and struggled in his enclosure, thinking he was in his bed at home. When he saw the car's headlights flood the tree line on the other side of the clearing, he relaxed.

Though it was odd, a car in the woods is less conspicuous to a city dweller than, say, the sudden appearance of a bear or bobcat. Anthony could have easily chalked it up to having wandered onto private property, then merely turned over and tried to fall back asleep. He knew that as long as the car didn't shine its headlights in his direction, he would be screened by the trees and bush around him. Contacting the new arrival was certainly out of the question, as it was more likely he'd get a shotgun barrel placed to his nose than a friendly, dead-of-night greeting.

The vehicle parked, its engine still rumbling, then a man got out and walked around to the trunk. Anthony couldn't make out what the man retrieved from the trunk, though it seemed bulky, as he struggled with it for some time. Curious, Anthony retrieved his camera and utilized its night vision capability to illuminate the scene that was unfolding only forty or so yards from his position.

It was an SUV, and it didn't take him long to figure out that there were two people. He probably didn't need the night vision for what happened next. A man was dragged toward the wooded area on the other side of the clearing, which was lit by the headlights, and then shot twice. Anthony tensed up in response, as a spike of adrenaline rushed through his body, painfully contracting every muscle, tendon, and ligament. He turned the camera off and slowly lowered his arms to his sides, as he was in immediate fear of revealing his presence.

Anthony lay stock-still in that hammock for a few quiet minutes, his clothes completely sweat-sodden, until he heard the unmistakable sounds of digging. The newly deceased was being given a burial, and each clang of the shovel against the rocky soil rang out as a warning to Anthony—that if he moved, or even flinched, he might be next. For Anthony, this could have gone on for forty minutes, it could have been two hours. It was an unending stretch of time that was only broken up by the reappearance of the skunks.

They were louder than before—scampering, fighting, screeching, lip smacking, gnawing, which grated at his senses. He dreaded that these foul-smelling creatures might draw more attention his way, and possibly lead to his discovery. He nearly puked in his hammock from the anxiety of it all.

Eventually, the shoveling did stop, and car doors were opened and closed as the shooter prepared to leave. Luckily, the vehicle backed up in Anthony's direction to turn around, and not vice versa. Had the driver illuminated Anthony's precarious position, he would've likely spotted the bulky hammock.

Anthony didn't get much sleep for the rest of that night. He kept listening for the return of the vehicle, the skunks, or even something unknown—the slain returning from his shallow grave to seek vengeance upon the living... Miraculously, the sun did come up that morning and Anthony quickly took down his hammock and secured his gear.

He only briefly considered leaving before satisfying his morbid curiosity. He told himself he'd just go and see the grave for himself, get a record of it on camera for the local cops, then be off. But Anthony didn't have to go far at all to find a shallow burial. A short distance from where he had slept, at the edge of the tree line that parted for the circular clearing, he found what the skunks had so furiously fought over the night before.

A thin, yellow bone lay in the dirt beside a protruding scapula, freshly dug from the ground, the chewing marks evident on the human remains. Anthony began filming, and he found grave after grave along the interior of the forest clearing. Bones of every shape and size imaginable littered the surrounding area. He shivered at the thought that he'd basically been suspended for an entire night over some mafioso's burial ground.

When Anthony got to the far side of the clearing, he found the grave which had been dug the night before. The area smelt of decay. The acrid, earthy scent, which he had only caught wafts of in the breeze, was now difficult to bear. He knew that this must be where the more recent burials had taken place.

Anthony didn't waste too much time recording what he had found. He was soon headed back down Bear Hole Brook, toward Peekamoose Road and his own car. The couple miles flew by and he was soon back in the parking area, packing up his car for the journey to any nearby town where he could contact law enforcement, or at least get a couple bars on his cell phone to call 911.

He was relieved to see an Environmental Conservation Police Officer decal on the door of an approaching vehicle.

"Hey, *hey!*" yelled Anthony, waving his arms.

The officer was already pulling into the parking area, and he stopped beside Anthony's car.

Anthony went over to the Jeep while the much older, clean-cut officer rolled down his passenger side window. "Sir, I was staying in the woods along Bear Hole Brook last night, and I found something terrible…"

"Is that right?" said the officer. "Are you sure you weren't partying all night at the swimming hole? I just found a real mess out there…"

"No, sir. I was camping overnight in the forest, and I found some bones and such."

The officer paused, taking in Anthony's unsettling information. "Get in, son. Let's go take a drive to my office in Sundown. It's not far."

Obeying the officer, Anthony got in the car and they pulled away. He took some comfort in the fact that the conservation officer was armed.

"So, you were staying along Bear Hole Brook and saw some bones?"

Anthony nodded, holding up his handheld to show the officer. "I even recorded it."

"It's likely deer remains," said the officer. "Most people can't tell the difference, and we end up sending a forensics expert out somewhere and they laugh at us for wasting their time."

"I think these are human remains," said Anthony. "In fact, I think I heard someone get shot out there last night."

Anthony looked for some sort of strong reaction from the conservation officer, but the man merely shook his head. "Christ. First the mess at the Blue Hole, now I have to deal with this. All before my second cup of coffee."

The officer then turned off the main road onto a dirt road, which eventually became nothing more than a rocky, dirt path. For a few minutes Anthony considered whether it was just a shortcut, but as the road became more of a trail, and the forest began to close in around the vehicle, he grew more and more uncomfortable.

"This isn't the way to Sundown, is it?" asked Anthony, his tone revealing his fear.

"No. I want you to show me what you found."

"I'd really prefer that we don't go back out there," said Anthony. "I can show you the video right now..."

The officer didn't reply. The SUV soon pulled out into a clearing, which was now all too familiar to

Anthony. He panicked as they came to a stop near the tree line. He tried to swallow but couldn't—his throat was still parched from his rushed hike back to the main road. Anthony looked around the vehicle for an escape, a weapon, an answer... Then he saw it. A shovel peeking out from beneath the second row of seats, with freshly dug soil caked to its tip...

"Son, I'm gonna need you to get out of the vehicle and start diggin' me a hole."

GHOSTS OF THURSTON AVENUE

"Since the early 1970s, nearly 30 people have jumped to their deaths from the Thurston Avenue Bridge, or 'Suicide Bridge' as it's commonly referred," said Laura Drucker.

The 35-year-old folklore professor stood before a class of fifteen Cornell graduate students, as photographs of the picturesque bridge were projected onto a screen at the front of the room. "Over the decades, various ghost stories and urban legends have sprung up around the site. How many of you are familiar with this grisly phenomenon?"

"I know all about it, Laura, I mean...Dr. Drucker," said Allen Rockland, a first-year doctoral candidate in folklore and mythology. "I had actually heard about it before I even arrived on campus, from an urban legend site I follow. People have seen ghost jumpers at the Bridge over the years. Some have reported that before the apparitions hit the bottom of the gorge, they vanish."

Laura nodded at her star pupil. "It's one of the more common legends. Stories like this have popped up in similar sites around the country, usually in or around college campuses. Most concern students who were so overwhelmed by their newfound freedom—stress over grades, being away from home for the first time, peer pressure—that they felt like their only choice was to end it all."

"Let's all hope that we pass this class," said Allen, sparking the class to a genial laughter.

When the lecture was over, a young, pert brunette approached Allen.

"Show-off," she said, smirking.

"What can I say, Maggie? I know my shit," said Allen.

Maggie went to kiss Allen on the cheek, but he recoiled.

"Not in class," said Allen, eyeing Professor Drucker, who was packing up her laptop. She waved at her two students before they left.

Allen and Maggie walked across campus together, which had become an autumnal wonderland, the trees radiant shades of red, yellow and orange. Allen slowed when they neared Thurston Avenue Bridge.

"Do we have to stop again?" said Maggie.

"You can keep going if you want," said Allen.

Maggie looked uneasily at the rocky gorge below. It was a dramatic drop. "That's a long way down."

"Yeah, nearly instant death," said Allen, excitedly. "One guy actually did survive; he ended up graduating."

"Lucky him," said Maggie. "Do you really believe in that ghost crap?"

Allen's expression flattened. "It's not 'crap.' I'm going to get footage of the phenomenon and prove it."

"Yeah?" Maggie didn't understand Allen's fascination with such grim subject matter. However, she did appreciate his passion and confidence. She took him by the hand and kissed him, and this time he kissed her back.

"Allen, I love you."

He pulled away and chuckled. "I told you to stop saying that. It's too serious. I like what we have."

"It's fine. I can wait," replied Maggie, sheepishly. They crossed the bridge and headed for her dorm.

"Holy shit," said Allen, flopping over onto the bed, exhausted, Dr. Laura Drucker beside him. It was evening, hours after he had dropped Maggie off at her room.

Laura got up and began dressing.

"You don't waste any time, do you?" said Allen. "You have a lecture to give or something?"

"It's almost 6:30. Roger will be back in the next hour."

"We've got plenty of time." Allen put on his boxers, then got out of bed and wrapped his arms around her torso.

"No, we don't," said Laura, brushing his hands aside. "You need to leave before my husband arrives."

"You want to come with me, over to Thurston Ave.?"

"What for?"

"I'm looking to catch a ghost."

"Ghost?" Laura smirked at her student and part-time lover. "No, I think I'll sit this one out."

After he had gathered his things and said goodnight, Allen left his paramour's home. Laura lived off campus, so by the time he reached the bridge, the temperature had dropped several degrees and a dread blackness had overtaken the sky. It was an atmosphere that Allen enjoyed, and made the whole prospect of capturing a ghost an even more pleasing venture.

The bridge led to a small forested area, where Allen set up his trail camera. He wrapped the camouflaged device around a maple tree, ensuring that the full length of the bridge was in view. He knew that documenting an actual paranormal event would bolster his reputation in academic folklore circles. When he had the camera in place, and adequately concealed from view, he left, certain that his investment would pay off. When triggered by movement, the camera took a photograph of the area every ten seconds, providing him a (mostly) uninterrupted view of the site. It was like having 24-hour access to Loch Ness or Chicago's Resurrection Cemetery.

Allen returned to the bridge each morning before class, accessing the previous nights' photos, disappointed in the results. He would briefly remove the memory card from the camera to load the photos onto his laptop, hoping that he had captured the phantom of a former student who had jumped to his or her death. There were images each time he checked the trailcam, just nothing out of the ordinary. Usually, it was a student or two walking home from an evening class, sometimes a group of frat guys hanging around and drinking, often a small woodland creature scampering down one of the railings. There was no sign of any spectral activity.

He'd told the urban legend message board he frequented about his plan, and they were excited about it, constantly asking for updates. Allen was frustrated that he didn't have anything to share with his fellow legend trippers, and wasn't about to post anything regarding his project to the online academic bulletin boards until he had something of note.

"Why don't you turn off the computer and come spoon me?" said Maggie. She lay nude in Allen's bed.

Allen had already put on his T-shirt and boxers and was reexamining some of the previous night's trail photos more closely. "I thought maybe I saw something in one of the photos, like a woman's face in the leaves of an oak tree; but I was just matrixing."

"I'm sorry it's not working out, Al." Maggie got out of bed and put on one of his button-ups, then came over to see what he was working on.

"I'll probably just go take it down later."

Maggie massaged his shoulders. "Give it a little more time. Maybe they only come out on certain nights or something."

"I don't know. Maybe."

"I'm sure you'll catch something." She smiled reassuringly. "How does the camera work anyway? I'm not really the technical type. You're a whiz at all that stuff."

"It's your typical trail camera. Whenever something passes the infrared sensor, it senses the movement— like a garage-door floodlight or an automatic door. Once it's triggered, it takes a photo every ten seconds until there's no more activity."

"Hmm. Maybe ghosts don't trigger infrared cameras," said Maggie, trying to be sympathetic. "Or, perhaps they trigger the camera, but disappear before the image can be captured."

"I really have no idea—but anything's possible, right?"

"Have you talked about any of this with Professor Drucker?"

Allen tensed at the mention of his other lover's name. "No, I'm not going to bother her until I have some sort of evidence. She's a leading scholar and I don't want to come off like some try-hard amateur."

"You talk about her like she's some sort of urban legend superstar. When really, she's just some random professor..."

Allen glared at Maggie. "You've got a problem with Laura?"

"*Laura?*" Maggie giggled. "I didn't know you were on a first-name basis."

"She's my advisor," snapped Allen.

"Okay, she's your advisor. But you're a smart, young scholar with big ideas and she's some no-name professor—on a campus full of academic superstars—whose best days are probably behind her—"

"Who the hell are *you*?" said Allen. "Laura's a brilliant academic; you don't know shit about any of this stuff."

Maggie's face twisted at her lover's sudden turn. "Why are you calling me names? I'm your girlfriend, and I'm just looking out for you."

"No, you're not. You're a *fucking fling*."

Maggie's lip quivered, and her eyes began to tear up. "You don't mean that..."

Allen let out a heavy sigh. "I can't do this anymore. You're a sweet girl and I have a good time with you, but I don't feel the same way about you as do you about me—not to mention, I'm in love with someone else..."

Maggie trembled, feeling as if she might crumple to the floor at any moment. She didn't say another word to Allen as she got dressed and left.

Allen hadn't been prepared for the flurry of emotion that would come with his rejection of Maggie. He stewed for hours in his room. She had set him off, but also inspired him to reveal his true feelings to Laura. It was already late into the evening, and he was certain that Laura's husband, Roger, would be home, but he felt an inextinguishable compulsion to knock on her door and say what needed to be said.

Laura opened the door and, before Allen could enter the house, she pushed him back onto the porch, closing the door behind her to conceal their conversation.

"What the hell are you doing here!" she said, her voice low but no less menacing. "My husband is in the living room!"

Although Allen knew he had made a rash decision in coming there, he was surprised to see his lover so cold to him, considering how close they had grown over the semester. "Laura, I needed to see you. I can't hold it in any longer. I've fallen madly in love with you over these past few months, and I had to tell you!"

"Allen, you have a profound misunderstanding of our relationship. I'm a married woman, going on twenty years, and I never intended on taking this any further than the dalliance it was."

Allen trembled at her cool, calm rejection of him. "You don't mean that. We have so much in common, Laura. I've never discussed urban legends, philosophy, and folklore as in depth with any other woman—we just...click. I know I'm a few decades younger than you, but I know we can make it work."

"You're a student. And that's where our relationship ends—advisor, student," said Laura, sternly. "I don't want you to contact me regarding anything but classwork going forward. Understand? And never show up at my house again. I'm going to have to explain to Roger why a student showed up at such a late hour."

Before Allen could plead with her, she shut and locked the door, leaving him alone on her doorstep.

Dejected, he walked to the Thurston Avenue Bridge and performed his daily ritual, removing the memory card from the trail camera and loading its contents onto his laptop. Allen considered bringing an end to his project but thought better of it. He still wanted to show Dr. Drucker that he was someone to be taken seriously. He knew that he would eventually capture a ghost, or a suicide, and have new evidence for a scholarly piece to present to the New York Folklore Society.

When he returned to his room, he scanned through the latest pictures, at first finding nothing but a few deer and the occasional student. But when he got to the last of the images captured that day, he spotted someone climbing the railing and protective fence. It was a young, brunette woman, and for a moment he was elated, that he had caught the legend playing itself out, another statistic to add to the growing list of casualties.

Allen returned to the first image of the woman and zoomed in; the girl's face and clothing were discernible as she approached. "It can't be..." he gasped. "Maggie!" The second photo already showed her climbing the railing, the third had her standing on the railing as she bent the flimsy fence back—and then nothing. He was horrified, made nauseous in discovering that Maggie had jumped following their argument.

He fled from his room to Maggie's dorm, wanting to be wrong. But after pounding on her door and calling for her, to no response, he accepted that the only place he might find her now was beneath the bridge.

Allen leaned over the railing, pressing his face into the fence, still hoping to God that he wouldn't see her body crumpled on a rocky surface below. He peered into the abyss, but it was much too dark to see anything. "Maggie!?" he shouted into the chasm. "Maggie!?"

He shook the useless fence and a pronounced rattling echoed throughout the gorge. He wailed and retched as he pondered all that he had lost that night. Laura. Maggie. And now, he was certain, his reputation and any chance at a future in academia. He had driven a cheery young woman to her death and had captured it all on camera for his macabre little picture show. No one would take him seriously going forward; he would likely be expelled.

Slowly, he ascended the railing, then pulled back the cold wire fence, as thirty or so kids had done before him...

Legends and Modern Folklore was cancelled the next morning, as were all Cornell classes, following the announcement of Allen Rockland's suicide. When class convened two days later, Laura Drucker approached Maggie, knowing that she had been close friends with Allen.

"I'm sorry for your loss," said Laura, as the class filed out of the room. "Allen was an excellent student with a bright future ahead of him. It's a... tragedy."

"Thank you, Professor," said Maggie, misty-eyed. "I'll really miss him. He was quite fond of you, you know."

"Is that so?" asked Laura, affecting a counterfeit look of surprise. "Well, I was fond of him too."

Laura said goodbye to Maggie and gathered her things. When she looked at the desk that Allen had occupied that semester, she felt a sense of relief. Roger had nearly discovered her relationship with Allen when she had left her phone unlocked a few nights prior, and after Allen had stopped by unannounced he had plenty of probing questions for her. She didn't want to wreck her marriage over a grad student and had promised him that she would better separate her work and home lives. She had enjoyed their brief fling but was relieved that her infidelity would now be forever concealed.

On the way back to her dorm, Maggie stopped on the Thurston Avenue Bridge and pondered the series of events that had led to Allen's untimely death. Angered by his rejection, she had decided to play a trick on him—to stand on the railing as if she were about to jump, trigger the trail cam, then jump down and run out of view of the camera during the ten-second window between shots. Maggie never would have believed that Allen would take his own life. Simply because she thought him too self-centered, too egotistical to be moved by the loss of a 'fling.'

She wept as she removed the trailcam from its perch, soon crushing the tiny memory card which had captured Allen's suicide, along with the evidence of her faux suicide. Maggie tossed the fragments over the railing and watched them flitter into the picturesque gorge below.

THE STAIRCASE AT WAVERLY GLEN

"Ricky, there's no way to even get over there," said Jeff Kazmark.

Two thirteen-year-old boys stood at a rusty fence beside a creek at Waverly Glen Park, staring at an old, decrepit staircase set into a wooded hillside. It was difficult to reach and appeared to lead to nowhere. Their families were picnicking at a pavilion by the playground, while they were off exploring the park.

"I'm telling you, they blocked the staircase off, so kids wouldn't try and walk up it," said Rick. "The creek was diverted, and they made this moat here because a fence wasn't enough."

"Sounds like horseshit to me, dude. Couldn't you just come down from one of the trails and go down it?"

Rick considered the logistics of it. "I don't think it works if you go down the stairs. I heard about kids climbing up them and disappearing."

"Why wouldn't they just remove the staircase then? Seems like that would be easier than building a moat."

"They did, Jeff. But the staircase always returns, sometimes in a different part of the park."

Jeff didn't have a rebuttal. Rick's stories about the disappearing kids of Waverly Glen were beginning to creep him out. "Where do you think you go, if you take the stairs?"

"Probably some witch's cottage, deep in the woods somewhere," said Rick, smirking.

"Well, don't get any dumb ideas. Our parents will have a shit-fit if they see us trying to cross the moat."

"I'm not saying we walk up the stairs. I just thought it'd be neat to get a closer look."

Jeff shook his head. "Yeah, right. Let's go check out the waterfall and lake. Did you bring your fishing pole?"

Rick nodded. The boys then returned to the picnicking area to grab lunch with their families.

"Hey, Dad. What's that for?" said Jeff, pointing to a concrete box along the pathway that led to the waterfall. It was raised two feet off the ground, with a ramp leading up to its flat top. Two exhaust pipes stuck out from the ground nearby.

Mr. Kazmark took a big bite of his hotdog and looked to what his son was pointing at. "I don't know." He got Rick's dad's attention and asked him the same question.

"It looks like an old, Cold War-era fallout shelter," said Tim, Rick's father. He was an engineer, so Jeff and his dad were willing to accept his explanation without question. "I was checking it out earlier. It says, 'private property' and 'no trespassing' on it. Seems pretty strange for someone to maintain the rights to a bomb shelter in the middle of a public park."

Rick and Jeff were immediately intrigued and ran over to check it out for themselves. They were disappointed to discover that the doors to the shelter were sealed over with concrete.

"How are you gonna use a bomb shelter if you can't get in it?" said Jeff.

"What if it belongs to Hal Maris—and this is where he hid his wife's body?" Rick was referring to an infamous local disappearance, one that had occurred before they were even born. A wealthy man was tried multiple times for his estranged wife's murder—but was ultimately exonerated—as no body was ever recovered.

"That'd be pretty frickin' creepy. Considering our kid sisters have been playing by it all day," said Jeff.

"Whatever. Let's get our poles and check out the reservoir."

Not far was the waterfall, which fed the creek that ran through the park. Beyond the waterfall was an earthen dam and reservoir. The boys climbed the dam with their fishing gear, only stopping briefly at the waterfall's overlook to toss a few rocks into the cascade. They then went down to the reservoir to cast their allotment of worms into the dark-blue water.

"Haven't even gotten a bite yet," said Jeff. They'd only been fishing for a half hour before they grew bored of it.

"Yeah, this sucks. Let's go check out some of the trails," said Rick.

The boys brought in their lines and secured their gear, then headed across the dam and into the forest, which blanketed the hillside above the park. The trails were poorly marked and often came to abrupt halts or crisscrossed into each other. Ricky led the way, always acting confident about the direction they should go when the trail markings became confusing.

"We should head back down. It's probably almost time to go," said Jeff. His tackle box was getting heavy and his pole kept catching on twigs and branches as they wandered through the forest.

"Okay. Follow me."

Rick had stayed on the trail up to that point, and, in Jeff's opinion, seemed to be going in the right direction, but then he left the well-worn path and began down the hillside.

"Dude, let's just stay on the trail," said Jeff.

"This is a shortcut. It'll take us right down to one of the playgrounds."

"You sure?" asked Jeff, nervous that his friend would get them lost long enough to piss off their parents.

"Yes. No matter what, we'll hit creek or park," said Rick.

The boys navigated some of the steeper, bushy areas with care. Ricky yelped when he got caught by a thorny vine, a few of the thorns scratching his right leg.

"I think I see the creek," said Jeff, relieved.

"Definitely sounds like it!" shouted Rick, who was now far enough ahead of his friend that he could no longer see him.

"Where are you?" Jeff called out when he'd lost sight of Rick. He paused when he came to a steep embankment, and was curious how Rick had gotten down, as a safe route wasn't evident.

"I'm down by the creek, Jeff. Just jump down. This is *so cool*."

Jeff laughed to himself as he considered the sort of morbid crap that amused his best friend. He figured he'd find Ricky poking a squirrel carcass with a stick or something. He dropped his tackle box and pole into some ferns, then jumped down to where the ground flattened out, near the edge of the concrete moat.

"Where you at?!"

Ricky didn't respond, so Jeff continued. He could see his little sister at some distance, standing at the top of a slide on the playground. His father seemed to be trying to coax her down.

"C'mon, Ricky. I think it's time to leave, and I'm not sure how to get across the moat..." Jeff paused when he saw it, immediately stricken with fear. He spied Rick's fishing pole, laying in the middle of the mystery staircase.

"Ricky, are you up there?" He slowly approached the ancient, crumbling stairs. Jeff scrambled up the hill and reached under the metal railing of the staircase, to grab his friend's fishing pole. There was no way he'd set foot on even a single step. He called out to Rick again, this time louder. When he did, he caught the attention of his dad, who immediately jogged over.

"What the *heck* are you doing over there, Jeff?" asked Mr. Kazmark. "Get Ricky and get back over here, right now. It's time to go."

"Dad, I don't know where Ricky went. I was following him, but now he's gone."

Mr. Kazmark could tell that his son was seriously frightened. "Christ, Jeff—stay right there. I'm getting Tim."

Jeff turned back to the stairs, looking for any sign of his friend. He shivered, certain that Rick had climbed that staircase, and was now gone, and no amount of searching was ever going to find him.

After a few weeks, all hope was lost, and the official search for Rick was given up. Jeff often returned to the park and walked the trails, contemplating the nature of the staircase, hoping he might find a clue to his friend's whereabouts. The adults had all but laughed at him when he told them his theory—that Rick had taken the stairs and been teleported somewhere else. At one point, Jeff even considered following his friend up the staircase—but ultimately, his fear got the best of him.

In the months and years following Rick's disappearance, a new legend emerged among the local kids who played at Waverly Glen. It was said that if you put your ear up to one of the exhaust pipes from the fallout shelter, you could hear a boy crying out for help.

PERNICIOUS FICTIONS

Ice tinkled indifferently in C.W. Montgomery's bourbon as Peter Geller read aloud a passage from his latest manuscript. The ice didn't bother Peter so much as Montgomery's tendency to chew on the cubes once he grew disinterested. The incessant popping between the bestselling author's teeth eventually disrupted Peter's flow, causing him to give up on his read and ask for notes—if only to interrupt Montgomery's grating habit.

"Let me have a look. I believe I jotted a few ideas in the margins of your text last weekend," said Montgomery.

Peter tapped his foot on the distressed hardwood floor while Montgomery leafed through his novel. Montgomery was the most accomplished member of the Speculative Writers' Workshop of Binghampton and had agreed to critique Peter's new story: a self-conscious whodunit in which a frustrated architect investigates the mysterious death of his friend and business partner. Peter thought the story to be his strongest to date and hoped that someone of Montgomery's stature would find it worthy of criticism.

Montgomery sat back in his chestnut leather armchair, ignorant to Peter's crushing anxiety; he had been successful for many years and had long-forgotten the self-doubt which fledgling writers often faced. Time passed slowly for Peter as Montgomery dipped his drink and focused his attention on the 50,000-word manuscript, tentatively titled "The Marlowe Murder." While Montgomery flipped typewritten pages, he swirled his glass in hand, smirking to himself from time to time, and mumbling additional commentary that he didn't deem fit for Peter's ears. A dull headache stirred within Peter's temples, greatly exacerbated by his associate's habits and mannerisms. It seemed evident that Montgomery had made no notes, and this fact ate at Peter. He rubbed his forehead, now feeling each cube strike against the confines of the empty glass.

Finally, Montgomery looked up and addressed Peter. "I can diagnose this…"

Peter took an eager step toward the man. "Yes?"

"Yes. It seems you're attempting a three-ring circus here, while you ignore the peripheral performances. Do your characters not have a breadth of life and experience beyond the plot points?" said Montgomery. "I don't feel like I'm living in this world… Have you read *All That Jazz?*"

Peter nodded politely, anticipating a more intimate discussion of his work—but it never came. By this point in the evening his irritation had grown legs. Montgomery's critique was about as general, and unhelpful, as any blog or article on writing he'd ever come across—and it was evident that his colleague hadn't even glanced at his manuscript up until that afternoon.

Peter stood silent as Montgomery redirected the conversation to his five-book paranormal-thriller series set in 1950s New Orleans. "Take book three of my series, for example. I brought the city *to life*. I made

Bettie and Bobby flesh and blood..." Montgomery droned on about his successes, his Amazon ratings for each book in the series, his future editions where he hinted at delving into the lore of the Bermuda Triangle. It was disheartening for Peter, to say the least. He was desperate for in-depth feedback, as a literary agent had recently shown interest in his work. His deadline for submitting her a shoppable manuscript was now only a week away and he had counted on gleaning some actionable advice from his capable colleague.

"Anyway, I told Paul Helling and Richard Marcik I'd go for a drink tonight in celebration of *All That Jazz* going top-ten on Amazon this week," said Montgomery. "Let me know how it goes with your agent. If she's not on the ball, I'm sure I can get your stuff in front of my people."

Peter seethed as he feigned appreciation and appropriately genuflected before the Great C.W. Montgomery; he now had to accept that Montgomery was a fount of false promises. He half-smiled at the thought of the celebratory drink with Helling and Marcik, who were usually the first to badmouth Montgomery when he was absent, which was often. Still, it didn't stop Peter from feeling a fool. He had genuinely believed that Montgomery had shown some interest in his story when he told him the synopsis at the last writers' meeting. Since they were putting out stories within the same genre, Peter had hoped that the older man might mentor him, or at the very least give him a gentle nudge in the right direction.

"I'll see you at Friday's meeting, then?" asked Peter as he readied to leave.

Montgomery shook his head. "Can't make it. I'll be on the first leg of my book tour. Albany on Friday, then

Utica, Rochester, and Buffalo through the weekend." The author rose to show his colleague out.

"Well, thanks again for your advice," said Peter dispassionately.

"The book needs *a lot* more time in the oven, okay? As it stands, I don't see any serious publisher giving it any consideration. I'll take another look when you've worked out the kinks, okay?"

Peter said goodnight and left Montgomery's stately Colonial Revival, taking the well-lit cobblestone walkway to his rust bucket '98 Ford Taurus parked along the curb.

He sat inside and pounded his fist on the wheel. It had taken all the restraint he could muster to not make a snide remark about Montgomery's failure to properly critique the manuscript, or to harangue him for his vainglorious segue into his own work. But to do so would have likely earned him removal from the writers' group, and he certainly didn't want to be on the bad side of someone with Montgomery's clout in the small world of indie publishing; it would certainly sound the death knell for his nascent writing career.

Over the next several nights, Peter pored over his manuscript, attempting to liven up dull description and inject some much-needed energy and verisimilitude into the murder scenes. He had counted on gaining at least *some* insight from Montgomery on specific scenes—something that might help shape the book into something more palatable to modern audiences. Instead he could only parse through the document and make slight adjustments here and there, nothing he felt truly added to the book in a meaningful way.

Montgomery's dismissal had only helped to sour his outlook on the story, and he hoped that his upcoming meeting with the rest of the writers' group would result in more constructive feedback. He uploaded his latest draft to the group's shared cloud drive, with a note indicating that he had little time to improve his manuscript, stressing how important it was that they provide him any critique they could, and to do so as soon as possible.

So, when he arrived at the meeting later in the week, he was anxious to hear what the others thought of his manuscript. The group met the first Friday of every month at the home of Serena Cupelo, whose debut sci-fi novel, *Ascendant Dust,* had been nominated for a Hugo Award in the mid-2000s, a fact that seemed to come up at every meeting. There also were Paul Helling and Richard Marcik, both of whom had seen more success than Peter—Paul's horror thriller *Butcher at the Lake* had recently received a five-star review from *Cemetery Macabre Magazine* and Richard's spec-fic podcast *Writin' Weird* had just celebrated its 100th episode. Rounding out the group was Tabitha Hill, who was in the middle of writing the conclusion to her *Necromancers & Netherworlds* series.

Peter made small talk and shared a cup of coffee with the other writers in Serena's cramped parlor. It was mid-October and noticeably chill in the house. Tabitha frowned when Peter commented that there weren't enough bodies in the room to be an efficient source of thermal radiation.

It took an effort that evening for everyone to get situated on the dated green sofas and chairs. Peter had hoped that they would get to critiques immediately, as the meeting only lasted an hour and a half, but everyone was focused on the only member who wasn't in attendance: Montgomery.

"We usually talk on Twitter about the latest episode of *Dr. Who*—but he hasn't tweeted anything for days," said Serena. "I hope he's not sick."

"He's probably just at his cottage up at Wolf Lake for the weekend, drunk out of his mind like Jack Torrance," said Richard. Paul snickered, patting his pal on the shoulder.

"He's had a ton of signings lately," said Tabitha. "Maybe he's at a convention."

"I don't know of any cons in the region that would make sense for someone of his stature," said Serena.

"He's on his book tour this weekend," said Peter, quietly. He was surprised that Richard and Paul hadn't known that, despite having had a drink with Montgomery earlier in the week.

But no one seemed to have heard him.

"He's probably in the City sweet-talking a receptionist into letting him up to the Norton Publishing offices," said Paul.

Everyone laughed, save for Peter.

"...*or* he's busy writing another bestseller," said Serena, who didn't appreciate open mockery of a man she deemed the best living genre writer in New York.

"Maybe," said Richard. "I'll give it to him—he can blast out books faster than Stephen King."

"Christ. He's on the first leg of his book tour this weekend!" said Peter, his frustration showing.

The group went silent for a few beats, shocked by Peter's tone.

"Okay... So, that's settled then," said Tabitha, breaking the awkward silence.

Peter checked the clock; half of the meeting had already passed and nothing of substance had been discussed, most importantly his manuscript. Ten minutes alone had been spent earlier discussing the latest Marvel movie while Serena passed out flavored coffee creamers. "Do you think we can get to critiques? It's already 8:30."

"Sure"," said Serena. She wasn't the biggest fan of Peter's work—at a meeting a few months back she had called his first chapter "meandering and tedious."

"Do you guys mind if we talk about "The Marlowe Murder," first? Like I said, my agent is going to look at it soon and I—"

"Yeah, yeah, Pete. We know," said Richard, smirking. "It's your *big break*."

Peter glared at Richard, before continuing. "...And I need all the honest criticism I can get."

"Didn't you have a one-on-one with C.W.?" asked Paul.

Peter sighed. "Yes, I did, but..."

"Then what do you need to talk to us for?" said Serena. "C.W. is one of the best editorial critics I've ever known. He really helped me work through the major issues in *Ascendant Dust*. I don't think I would have had a *chance* at the Hugo nomination if it weren't for his analysis."

"Are you still planning a sequel?" asked Paul while making eye contact with Richard. It had been a running gag between the two men at each meeting, to bring up the fact that it had been a dozen years since Serena's first, and only, release.

"Not to brag or anything, but it's still moving really well," said Serena. "I'm just worried that General Kleeg might be a problematic character in this political climate. Sure, the story takes place in a different galaxy, but even archetypical Nazis can be triggering."

"If you need any help with that, let me know," said Tabitha. "*Necromancer Dawn* was originally a stand-alone story, but it was so well-received by the grimdark community I figured out a way to build upon the mythos without putting off my original fanbase."

Peter made several attempts to steer the discussion back to his manuscript, but there was no clear break in the conversation that would allow him to do so without coming off as a prima donna. Talk then turned to cosplaying, and everyone aside from Peter agreed to dress as the cast of *FarScape* at the next big con. Peter shifted on the sofa, sighing openly.

"Is something wrong, Pete?" asked Paul.

"No," said Peter. He didn't want to waste another minute. "So, what did everyone think of my chapter 15 changes? I tried to make Josh a little more sympathetic with the little blurb about his upbringing, but I'm not sure that it works in context."

"Which one is Josh again?" asked Serena.

"Uh...the lead character," replied Peter.

"Oh," said Serena.

"To be honest, Peter, I didn't get a chance to read it," said Richard. "Editing the podcast just ate up so much of my time this week. I couldn't squeeze it in."

"But you *had* time to 'squeeze in' *Iron Man 4*," said Peter, without a hint of playfulness.

"*Iron Man 4* doesn't exist," said Paul, chuckling.

Richard snickered. "Yeah, man. It was the third *Thor* movie."

Everyone else in attendance either stared uncomfortably at the floor or giggled awkwardly in response to Peter's abrupt comment. When Richard rolled his eyes and whistled, it only emboldened Peter.

"Did *anybody* read my story? Can *anyone* offer me an ounce of feedback? You all knew how important this critique session was for me. I've been at every meeting and have read all your work and offered my thoughts. I think it's only fair that you do me the same courtesy."

"We have, Pete," said Serena. "You've been tinkering with that murder mystery of yours for ages now, and I don't blame anybody for not wanting to go over the same passages *again and again*. You should be happy someone like C.W. took time out of his day to read it and offer feedback."

"She's right," said Tabitha. "You should be grateful. C.W's latest has been in the top 10 of your genre for weeks now. He's clearly doing something right. I'd take his advice, if I were you."

"C.W. didn't read it either!" said Peter, disrupting the low-key ambiance of the room. He then stood abruptly and stared down each member of the group. "I could have gotten better feedback from my accountant at H&R Block."

Richard and Paul laughed nervously.

"Peter! I won't have you talk like that in my home, and *especially* about a close friend."

Peter rolled his eyes. "Oh, we mustn't talk poorly of the exalted C.W. Montgomery. May Odin of the MCU strike me down."

"You've insulted everyone here who took the time to read your mediocre murder mystery over the past six months!" barked Serena. "It's time for you to leave."

"Gladly," said Peter, now oddly sedate as he left the cold parlor for the crisp autumn air. As he exited to the city street, he told himself that the group was nothing more than a social club. That he had, and would, steadily improve his craft without them.

Peter bore down on his manuscript over the weekend, plugging away at his story from Saturday morning until Sunday evening, fueled by bologna sandwiches and a steady stream of K-Cup coffee. He emailed his manuscript to his prospective agent before bed that

Sunday and waited patiently that week for her response.

Peter's day job was running deliveries for a uniform and rug cleaner, and when he returned to his company depot that Thursday afternoon, a police detective was waiting to speak with him.

"You're Peter Geller?" asked the detective.

"Yes," said Peter.

"I'm Detective Stimak." He offered his hand to Peter and they shook. "Your boss said we could use his office to chat. Is that alright?"

Peter had seen enough YouTube videos to know why one should never talk to the police. "What's wrong?"

The detective seemed to be caught off guard by Peter's hesitancy. "I don't know if you've heard, but Christopher Wellington Montgomery was murdered."

"What? Where?"

"Can we discuss this in the office?"

"Yes."

Peter followed Detective Stimak into his boss's shoebox office and closed the door behind him.

"I've been trying to track down members of your writing group, to see if anyone knows why he would've been targeted," said Stimak. "He never arrived at his book signing last Friday, and his agent contacted his sister. She was the one that discovered him after a lengthy search."

"Oh, Christ... What happened?"

"He was found strangled at his cabin on Wolf Lake," said Stimak, habitually looking over Peter's grease-stained hands. "It was a struggle."

Peter sighed. Internally he was anxious, but also moderately gleeful. A mix of emotion he wasn't proud of but had become accustomed to feeling during tragedy.

There was something about a horrible situation that gave him a pleasurable sense of relief. That he wasn't the one murdered, yes, but also that something intriguing was taking place to liven his every day, humdrum existence.

"You met with Montgomery last week?"

The detective's voice pulled Peter from his navel-gazing. "Yeah. We were discussing my new mystery novel."

The detective took down the times that Peter arrived and left Montgomery's, making small notes in his scratchpad as Peter gave a brief synopsis of his and Montgomery's relationship, even about Peter's work in progress.

"A few of the guys at the station have read some of Montgomery's books," said Stimak. "They say he was really talented."

Peter gritted his teeth, as had become second-nature to him over the months and years when Montgomery's success was brought up as a novelty, while the content of the man's ideas, characters, and plotlines went unexamined.

After the detective left, a wave of nauseous anxiety overtook him. He knew he was a suspect in Montgomery's murder, and had likely made his situation worse—despite knowing that one should never accommodate a police investigation, regardless of one's guilt or otherwise.

Peter entered the bathroom and went into a panic attack. He scrubbed his dirty palms with the special gritty soap while watching his face pale and beads of sweat run from his temples. He kicked himself when he realized that hadn't mentioned that Paul and Richard were supposed to meet Montgomery for a drink. He considered contacting the detective but felt that it might make his position worse. After all, someone in the writing group may have made it a point to tell the detective that he had been the last person to see Montgomery alive. It very well could've been Paul and Richard fingering him. And then there was Serena, who would certainly let Stimak know, through overzealous tears, about Peter's outburst at the writers' group.

Peter stopped at the Union Hotel bar, and then again, the next night after work, and so on. He let his anxiety eat away at him, forgetting about whether his agent cared for his story. He was now waiting on Detective Stimak's phone call. He'd certainly be questioned again. Maybe even charged and arraigned before long. What if he really was the last to see the minor celebrity C.W. Montgomery alive?

Peter couldn't help but read the news daily, following along with the story and investigation. He dreamed of Montgomery's garroting, the struggle, as if he bore witness to the shambles of the cottage. He wondered why he hadn't ever been invited to Wolf Lake for a writers' pow-wow like some of the other authors in the group.

What was it about him that especially repulsed Tabitha and Serena? Why did Paul blow off his apt criticism of the passive-voice narrative in Paul's story "Death by Digitalis"? Was it because they all worked in professional positions for their day jobs, while he paid his bills by way of his sweat and toil?

*   *   *

It was late one evening at the Union Hotel. Peter was inebriated, slumped over his Blanton's bourbon whiskey. He had taken to Blanton's after having seen Montgomery drinking that brand. It felt like the more authentic Kentucky bourbon to him. That a writer would prefer Blanton's over Jim Beam. But never with ice. No ice in his drink, like on the Continent. He had never been to Europe, but he had heard they never put ice in their drinks.

"Hey, Geller!"

Peter looked up, finding Paul and Richard approaching him in the empty bar.

"You two!" sputtered Peter. "You told the detective, didn't you?"

Paul and Richard separated and bent over each of Peter's hunched shoulders for a private chat.

"Settle down, big guy," said Richard.

"Relax, relax," said Paul, patting Peter's back. "Let's have a drink."

Peter couldn't tell if he was smelling the alcohol on his own breath or if the other men were just as gone as him, but their glassy eyes hinted at the latter.

"Didn't you two meet up with Montgomery?"

"Last week?" asked Richard.

"Nah, he blew us off," said Paul.

"Really? Huh. Still, that's a real low move to point the finger at me," said Peter.

"What do you mean by that, Pete?" asked Richard.

"You guys told the detective I was the last to see him alive," said Peter. "I guess now I'm the number one suspect."

"Why would you think that, pal?" said Paul, awkwardly massaging Peter's shoulder.

Peter shook him off.

"What's wrong, Pete? You don't have to compete with the likes of Montgomery anymore," said Richard. "You should call Montgomery's agent, since you're writing in the same space."

Peter looked over each man, confused at what their angle was. "Why'd you say something as shitty as that, Dick?"

Richard grimaced at the nickname. "Listen, peckerhead, we *did* read your little story."

"Yeah, it's quite the twist having the guy who's investigating the crime be the murderer," added Paul.

"Serena and Tabitha made the connection too," said Richard.

"What the hell are you guys getting at?" said Peter. He choked his glass, ready to smash it into either of their faces.

"It is a bit cheesy, having the architect kill his friend and colleague over an artistic rivalry," said Paul.

"Strangulation with a belt even," said Richard.

"Yep, Montgomery was strangled to death with a belt," said Peter. He attempted to stand but was kept on his stool by the two hands planted firmly on his shoulders. "Gimme a fuckin' break..."

"Sure, Montgomery was a lauded hack," said Paul. "But you didn't need to *kill* the guy."

"Yeah, he had pretty long coattails, which we all benefited from," said Richard. "Even you, whether you knew it or not."

Peter pushed his way out of the grasp of the other two men, surprising them. He headed for the door while Paul and Richard trailed close behind.

"Montgomery never did shit for me," stated Peter, before looking back. "And that's a fact."

When Peter stepped out into the alley Richard and Paul surprised him by pinning him to the brick wall behind the dumpster. At first, he didn't fight them, as he had hoped to surprise them again as he had at the bar.

"That's funny. He said he'd let his agent look at your manuscript," said Paul. "He wouldn't do that for me when I was shopping *Butcher at the Lake*."

"Yeah, like he actually meant it..." said Peter, staring back at Paul. "Wait, how the hell do you know that?"

"What?" asked Paul.

"Forget this guy," said Richard, removing his hands from Peter and taking a step back. He bumped into the dumpster and a large metal rod fell to the ground with a *clang*.

Peter knew he was onto something, regardless of his level of stupor. "You jerks did have a drink with Montgomery that night! How else would you know what we talked about?"

Paul looked briefly to Richard, before slugging Peter in the mouth. Peter slumped down against the wall to a sitting position.

"Let's just go, Paul," said Richard. "Someone might be watching."

"Dick, I can't imagine you strangling a man with your belt," said Peter. "Did you just watch?"

Paul kicked Peter in the stomach. "Shut up!"

Peter crumpled to his side, now tasting blood from the earlier punch. Richard was caught in the headlights when Paul looked back at him. He didn't know if he should pull Paul away, let him continue, or just run himself.

Paul saw his friend's inaction, and considered leaving with him, but then Peter spoke: "You guys were fishing for information? Wanted to know what I told the cop?"

"N- no, not at all..." said Richard, wavering.

Peter spit up some blood. "You don't sound very convincing, Dick."

Richard's comments and Peter's mocking infuriated Paul. He looked around for a moment, then picked up the metal rod. Without hesitating, he struck Peter square in the face with a grotesque *thud*. Blood splattered against the brick above Peter, who now lay motionless.

"God, why'd you do that?!" exclaimed Richard.

Paul was huffing, breathing heavy. He looked down at the rod and then at the trickle of blood that ran down Peter's forehead. "He wouldn't shut his mouth."

"Let's go," said Richard, who had quickly sobered up to what had taken place. "Bring the rod."

The two men ran off, leaving Peter in the alley to die.

*   *   *

"This is insane," said Serena. "Two local authors dead, and they haven't found the murderer."

"I heard that they don't think the deaths are related," said Tabitha.

Serena and Tabitha sat in the rear of the Coleman Funeral Parlor chatting, after having gone through the line at Peter Geller's viewing.

"Well, I hope not," said Serena. "Imagine if there's a serial killer targeting the Speculative Writers' Workshop..."

"I highly doubt it." Tabitha smirked. "Hey, I ran into Peter's agent earlier."

"Yeah?"

"She's high on Peter's novel," said Tabitha. "She says St. Martin's is interested in buying it."

"No way! They're huge," said Serena.

"It's a shame," said Tabitha. "He got exactly what he wanted—what he thought he deserved—and didn't live long enough to enjoy it."

DEATH IN THE FAMILY

I was studying at the local junior college when my dad had his stroke. My mother paged me on my beeper, but it was too late. I'm still not sure why she took so long to let me know that Dad had been admitted. But by the time I got to the hospital, he was gone.

I can't say that my mother and I had any kind of real relationship after I had moved out, but my dad and I sure did. He had managed the movie theater right across from my college, The Cameo Multiplex. I stopped by to see him almost every day, and at least twice a week we'd see a movie together. Every little girl absolutely adores her daddy, then puberty hits and relationships change. But for me it was different; there had been no depreciation in that perfect childhood love that I'd always had for him. He was a frequent presence in my dreams in the weeks following his death. Never nightmares, just bittersweet imaginings that led to tears when I awoke and was forced to accept reality.

After weeks of mourning my father I attempted to move on with my life. I shared an apartment with another girl who went to my school, and we partied harder than I'd like to admit. I went out on dates, did my coursework, and was sending applications to far-flung universities. There was no reason for me to hang around Binghampton anymore. My mother wasn't a part of my life at all. Daddy and I had tried to get her to go to rehab for years, but she was stubborn and completely addicted.

I barely said two words to her during the funeral. Our relationship was so far gone that we no longer even bothered to argue. Luckily, my Aunt Kathy handled all the details for the service and burial, with some minor input from me. My mom had been hungover at my father's viewing and reeked of alcohol during the burial. We could all smell her. Most everyone had given up on her after years of trying to help. She rarely left the house, as her license had been suspended for over a decade. I felt like she had betrayed my dad by not getting help. He had taken care of her while working long hours and raising me. He never made excuses for her, never aided her addiction in any way—beyond loving her for who she once was. He had never ceased hoping and praying that she would work toward sobriety of her own accord. Now he was dead, and I was moving on.

I found myself returning to The Cameo week after week, right on schedule for new releases. I liked to visit with the people who had worked for my dad, to hear them talk about him, always with fondness. I had one early class and the rest of my college schedule took up my afternoons, so I could usually make the first showing for the day. It was a treat having the theater to myself for the smarter movies—the limited-run dramas, and indie films that never ran for more than a couple weeks. I was a bit of a movie snob but found myself watching the big blockbusters that my dad would have enjoyed. He liked the indie films too, but there was nothing he loved more than big explosions—especially within the context of a heroic war drama.

It was during a showing of a new military picture that I first felt the chill of being watched. It was a guy I had seen in passing the week before. I remembered him because he wore an old green parka with the hood up and a knit hat underneath, even though it was warm inside the theater. The first time I saw him he had sat in the back, but now he was only a few rows behind me.

I knew he was watching me because he was wearing sunglasses and we were the only two people in the theater. For the remainder of the picture I remained vigilant and didn't get to enjoy the film. I was worried that he might approach me.

I was relieved when he left just before the end of the movie. When it was over I went out to the lobby and asked around to see if anyone had seen the man before.

"Yeah, I see him in the theater just about every day now," said Rodney, my dad's former assistant manager. "I think he gets his tickets from the kiosk. He usually doesn't talk to anyone. Just some loner, I guess."

"Is he always bundled up like that? Sunglasses and everything?"

"Yep. No idea what his issue is," said Rodney, who was distracted by a ticket taker waving him over. "Well, it's always nice seeing you, Julia. I've got to deal with this."

I said goodbye to Rodney and eventually forgot about Parka Guy, figuring he was merely some eccentric with time to kill.

I didn't go back to the theater for a week because I had finals to study for. But after I took the last test for my morning class, I went and saw the new John Cusack drama. Halfway into the movie I noticed someone coming down the aisle. I usually sat in the center of a row; that way no one would have to cross in front of me.

I had only seen two couples in the theater for that showing, so I was shocked when Parka Guy sat in the row behind me. There was no entrance behind me, so I didn't know how this guy could've come in without me knowing. I sunk as far down into my seat as I could, while this Unabomber look-alike stared at the back of my head through his dark glasses.

It became too distracting, and moderately un-nerving, knowing he was right behind me. Though I was enjoying the film, I got up and left at the halfway point. I hung around the lobby to see if Rodney was around, because I wanted to chat with him about Parka Guy creeping up on me, but the concessions manager, Amanda, said he was busy doing payroll and wouldn't come out of his office for a couple more hours.

I eventually returned to the theater to finish the film I had walked out on. I was relieved when Parka Guy made no appearance. However, Rodney stopped me in the lobby on my way out with this odd look on his face, like he was conflicted about what he was about to tell me.

"Julia, I'm not sure if you dropped this the other day, or if it was left for you..." Rodney handed me a folded piece of paper which had 'Julia' neatly written across it. It was sealed with a pink heart sticker.

"I didn't drop it. You don't know who left this for me?" I asked, anxiously taking the letter.

"The cleaning crew found it in Theater 6 the other day," said Rodney. "Amanda said you left a movie early that morning, so I assumed it was for you."

My chest tightened as I peeled off the sticker and opened the trifold paper. I knew exactly who had left it behind.

I scanned the brief note and then read it to Rodney: "*Stay safe. He's always watching.*"

"So, you didn't bring this in with you?" asked Rodney. He had a grave look to him then, and I noticed that he was sweating through his shirt.

"No. I'm assuming it's from Parka Guy." I practically whispered it, so no one would overhear.

"Oh, Christ. That's what I was worried about," said Rodney as he pulled at his starched white collar. "We can't go six months without having some type of stalker or flasher coming through here..."

"You think Parka Guy is stalking me?" I asked, now frightened. My first thought had been that he was just some regular creep. But now I began to consider whether he would be watching me outside of the confines of the theater.

"Julia, I promise you I'll confront him the next time I see him," said Rodney, who was now bristling. "I'll make him take off his hood and put the sunglasses away, and I'll tell him to leave you alone or don't come back!"

I stayed away from the theater for some time. Only when the school semester was over did I go back. I had time to kill and the feeling of nostalgia I got whenever I visited The Cameo was too powerful to ignore. I was supposed to attend a Christmas party at my Aunt Kathy's that evening and was already dressed for the occasion, as I was planning on traveling to her house after the movie got out. I was wearing a cute red-and-green striped dress, and I felt a little out of place as I walked through the theater lobby to purchase my ticket.

"You look great, Julia," said Rodney, swimming through a crowd of moviegoers to hug me. He asked me how my final tests had shaken out and if I was meeting up for a date, because of how pretty I was dressed.

"Nope, just a party tonight at my aunt's."

Rodney saw that I was looking around nervously, so he leaned in to whisper: "Julia, I haven't seen you-know-who around since we discovered the letter."

"Oh, that's good," I said, relieved. I wished Rodney a Merry Christmas and soon found myself sitting in my usual row in Theater 6, ready to digest the latest holiday-themed romantic comedy.

The movie was what I expected—passably entertaining schmaltz. I had to use the restroom during the movie, something I always loathed doing. After I had relieved myself and returned to my seat in the packed theater, I was shocked to find a letter with my name on it in the cupholder. I snatched up the paper, swallowing a lump that had formed in my throat when I realized that it was sealed with a pink heart. I shoved the note in my jacket pocket and crouched down in my seat. I slowly looked around, trying not to draw attention to my search. I began shaking when I spotted that all-too-familiar green parka, and those big black sunglasses in the section to my left. Parka Guy was undoubtedly looking in my direction, as he was sitting parallel to me.

My palms were sweaty as I grasped the armrests on my seat. It was disgusting, the sticky mix of sweat and popcorn grease. I wanted to get up and run; but I knew the best course of action would be to leave the theater as quietly as I had done when I went to the bathroom. I worried that any sudden movement on my part might cause my stalker to panic and possibly attack me.

My nerves fastened me to that chair for another couple of minutes. My brain was screaming at my legs, trying to get them to function. I recalled how my psychology professor once said that most people believe they will run or fight when confronted with a dire situation, when in truth, many will freeze and not act in their own defense. However, I wasn't one of those people.

I stood slowly, then hustled down the aisle, heading for the exit. Out of the corner of my eye, I thought I detected someone else standing as I fled. The hallway outside of the screening rooms was long. I kept looking back and saw him as he exited the theater. Parka Guy was following me!

I ran the remainder of the hallway and burst out into the busy lobby. I spied Rodney behind the ticket counter and ran right over to him, feeling safe that there were dozens of people nearby, including a man whom I knew personally.

"Rodney, he's following me!" I'm sure I looked and sounded like a lunatic to the dozen or so people that were waiting patiently to get their tickets. But Rodney understood immediately.

"Which theater?" asked Rodney as he shuffled out from behind the circular counter.

"He's in the hallway!" I pointed behind me.

Rodney rushed through groups of people who were milling about, waiting for theaters to empty. He returned minutes later, out of breath.

"He must've gone back in the theater, Julia," said Rodney. "You better get going. I promise that he won't get past me."

"Thanks, Rodney." I hurried out into the parking lot and got into my car.

When I turned my beeper back on I saw that I had gotten a call from Aunt Kathy. I was headed to her house anyway, so I just got on the road and started driving. I figured if she needed me to pick something up I could just head back out. I was in no mood to hang around and use the payphone at the theater.

Twenty minutes later I pulled into my aunt and uncle's driveway. There were already a few cars in the street, even though the party wasn't supposed to begin for another hour. I was about to get out of the car when I heard the paper crumple in my jacket pocket.

I pulled it out then flicked away the small heart seal. This note was as brief, and cryptic, as the last one: *I wish we could talk. I have so much to say to you.*

I couldn't help but wonder what this man might want from me. Did he really think that I'd go out and have coffee with him? That we'd have such a great chat we'd start dating and I'd fall for him? He was a creepy, stalking, sunglasses-wearing loser!

While I was getting myself all riled up, I didn't notice that my uncle had come up to the car window. I practically jumped out of my skin when he knocked on the glass.

Uncle Will seemed upset. I rolled down the window, and he fumbled, and barely spit out the news: my Aunt Kathy had found my mom dead in her house when she went to pick her up for the Christmas party. Kathy had been trying to get ahold of me.

I didn't let Uncle Will finish. I raced across town to my mom's house. When I arrived a few police cars and an ambulance were parked out front. I barely got my car into park before I rushed inside. The nearest cop attempted to shield me from the scene, but I tore my arm away and went into the living room, where my aunt and some medical folks were huddled around talking.

On a stretcher on the floor, her face covered with a white sheet, lay my mother.

"My God, Julia. She killed herself!" said Aunt Kathy. Her eyes were red from crying.

I surprised myself that I remained unemotional, as I wanted to know all the facts before I let myself feel anything.

The medics picked up the stretcher with my mom and I stopped them, so I could look under the sheet.

"Don't, Julia!" said Aunt Kathy.

It was too late. I saw her withered, pale expression. It was horrific—eyes open, mouth agape. She was a husk of a person, a shade of the woman who had at one time loved me, cared for me—before she had abandoned her duty for the bottle.

"How long has she been dead?" I asked the man with the medical examiner's badge who was standing beside my aunt.

"Weeks. Maybe longer," he said. "We'll do a full autopsy."

I collapsed on the sofa and began weeping at the thought of my poor mom's body rotting away in the living room for who knows how long. My aunt consoled me, held me as I cried.

When everyone had gone, Auth Kathy showed me my mother's suicide note. It read: *Julia, I wish we could talk. I have so much to say to you. But your father probably said it all, better than I could ever hope to. Stay safe. He's always watching.*

It was only then that I noticed the heavy, green parka draped across the far end of the sofa.

THREE-COURSE SCORCH

The Buffalo Wing Emergency Room was a new pub, quietly making a name for itself in the crowded metropolitan bar scene of Buffalo, New York. Its slogan was: 'If you haven't been to the ER, you haven't tasted hot!' Business was respectable in the few months that the bar had been opened, but co-owners Richie and Vinny Marino felt that they needed to do more to get their name out and better establish their brand. They were competing against some of the oldest bars in Buffalo, nationally renowned restaurants like the Anchor Bar and Wellington Pub, and they had to do something special if they wanted to pull customers away from these decades-old establishments.

To carve out their own niche, the Marino Brothers were marketing an eating challenge which they had dubbed the Three-course Scorch. To win, an entrant had to eat three successive plates of Buffalo wings, each flight hotter than the last, without aid of a beverage. Most didn't make it to the second plate. Richie and Vinny knew they had to go big, so they advertised that the winner of the challenge would win $1,000. That amount of money generated quite the buzz in the greater Buffalo area.

Scores came in to attempt the challenge; most were college-aged guys and older men who had lost most of their taste buds to decades of smoking. At $30, the entrance fee pricey, but this guaranteed the loser would still get their money's-worth if they couldn't finish all three plates. The restaurant would give out vouchers for the number of wings that weren't finished, but playfully, only allowed the losers to get these consolatory wings in a mild Buffalo sauce.

One Friday night, a group of college kids from Buffalo State came in to support their friend Mike in his attempt at the Three-course Scorch.

"What do you say, Mikey? You gonna win that money and buy our beer for the next couple months?" said Steve, one of Mike's roommates.

"After I win the challenge, you guys should buy *me* beer for a month," stated Mike. "No one has even come close, from what I've heard."

Vinny Marino came to the table to take the guys' orders. "I hear one of you wants to do the Scorch?"

"Yep. What are the rules?" asked Mike.

Vinny quickly explained the basics. "We'll bring out a plate of ten wings one at a time, and you've got to clean each one without taking a drink. Once the three plates are finished, you can drink all the milk or beer you want."

"Are you guys gonna be on the ball, and not make me wait between plates?" said Mike.

"My brother Richie will have the wings made," said Vinny. "You just eat 'em. We usually don't bother pre-saucing the third plate, since most people don't make it halfway through the first."

"Well, I can guarantee you that I'm making it through all three plates; so, you had better get that thousand dollars ready for me to take home tonight!" said Mike, cocky as ever. His buddies laughed and slapped him on the back.

"We'll see, my man," said Vinny. "Now, what do you other guys want?"

Vinny took the orders and went back to the kitchen.

"Richie, we're gonna need a plate for the Scorcher," said Vinny. "Got a kid out there talkin' like our challenge is nothin'. Make 'em extra special for him."

Richie Marino merely winked at his older brother as he finished a ticket behind the line, handing two platefuls of wings and calzones to one of the waitresses. Vinny gave him the new ticket and returned to the dining room.

"Joey, how many times do I have to tell you not to drive that thing in here!" yelled Richie. "I'm gonna bust that damn car."

Joey Marino, Vinny's twelve-year-old son, spent most evenings at his family's pub. He'd just gotten a new RC Monster Truck for his birthday and had been testing it out in the halls and backrooms of the Buffalo Wing Emergency Room. Richie had a short fuse. He ran his kitchen like an Army platoon and would cuss his nephew out if he dared step foot behind the line, where he and his cooks fired steaks and grease-fried finger foods.

"Sorry, Uncle Richie," said Joey. "I'm still learning the controls."

"You're gonna have to learn how to put it back together when I smash it with my tenderizer." Richie smirked, holding up a mallet as his nephew ran out of the kitchen, carrying the RC car.

Ten minutes later Vinny returned, and like clockwork, Richie had the complete order ready for the college kids, including Mike's first plate of the Three-course Scorch. "The wings are making my eyes water! You've done well, *paisan.*"

Vinny took the plates to the table of college guys, placing the first plate of the challenge in front of Mike with little fanfare. Mike took one last swig of beer, cracked his knuckles, then dove into the first ten hot wings.

"You got it, bro," said Steve. "Christ, you're not even breaking a sweat!"

Mike had plowed through the first five wings, completely stripping the meat to the bone, even taking down some of the cartilage as he went to work. His friends cheered him on. Vinny watched close by, amused.

"My man, let's get that second plate over here!" said Mike, before devouring the final two wings.

Vinny gave him a thumbs-up and headed to the kitchen. "Richie! This kid's a ringer. Must not have taste buds or something. Let's amp it up with plate two."

Richie was clearly irritated by the news. He huffed and puffed and tossed dishes around as he sauced a new plate of wings, adding a little more of his special extract than he normally would.

"Damn, Vin. I gave that last plate a little extra kick, like you said," stated Richie. "Don't sweat it, don't worry about it. Taste buds won't matter when he gets some of this shit in his mouth."

Richie finished saucing the second plate of wings for the challenge, handing it off to his brother. As soon as Vinny had stepped out to deliver the order, Joey's monster truck came tearing in through the bar service door, crashing into a garbage can. Richie punted the truck back through the door.

"I'm sorry, Uncle Richie! Please don't bust up my truck." Joey pleaded from the barroom as the swinging door closed.

Meanwhile, Vinny was growing ill, watching Mike strip wing after wing, which his brother had drizzled with capsaicin extract. Chemically, it didn't get much hotter than that. Vinny was dumbfounded. The kid had an iron mouth, esophagus, stomach—the whole shebang. Vin knew that part of the allure of the challenge was its difficulty. Once this kid had trounced it, people would lose interest. Talk and excitement about the bar and the challenge would wane. He would hate to lose $1,000 cash, but it would be far costlier to the Buffalo Wing Emergency Room's bottom line if Mike were to win the challenge.

"You got it, Mikey," said Steve. "You're making those wings your bitch! They're gonna have to change their slogan to: 'If you haven't been to the ER, then you're probably good eating at any other bar in town.'"

Mike and his pals busted out laughing, embarrassing Vinny, who was still standing nearby. Sure, Mike was sweating by now, his face beginning to flush, but his pace had barely diminished as he plowed through the final three wings of the second challenge plate.

"I'm on it. I'm on it," said Vinny, waving off Mike and his friends before they could demand the third, and final, plate.

"Richie, this kid's a machine," said Vinny, as he tore into the kitchen. "This is real bad. He's going through them like they're nothing. We're gonna have to shitcan the challenge once he beats it and come up with some new gimmick. *Christ!*" Vinny kicked the trash can.

Richie couldn't believe it. He had studied what the other wing challenges around the country had done wrong. He was a connoisseur of extreme heat, knew practically every pepper eaten by man. He saw how dejected and upset his brother had become, and now he, himself, was quickly becoming infuriated.

"*No fucking way* is some college kid gonna take down our challenge!" exclaimed Richie, pounding his fist on the service table. "Give me a few minutes, Vin. I'll think of something."

"Okay, okay." Vinny threw his hands up and went back out to the dining room.

Truth be told, Richie was out of ideas. He had gone right to his special blend of capsaicin extract on the last plate of wings, something he had only planned on bringing out if a third plate was ever needed for the Three-course Scorch challenge.

"*Fuck!*" Richie was tossing bowls and plates again. His cooks knew to make themselves scarce when he began to rage.

At the most inopportune time, Joey's RC truck tore into the kitchen from the back office, smacking Richie in the shin, painfully. "You motherfucker!" In one swift motion, Richie picked up the truck and smashed it against the back of the industrial stove. Plastic flew everywhere; the truck was now in pieces.

Joey stood in the doorway, terrified at what his uncle might do, as if smashing his new truck wasn't punishment enough. "I'm- I'm sorry, Uncle Richie. I was trying to park it in the office under my dad's desk and..."

Richie merely raised his finger and Joey stopped speaking. Joey was shocked when his uncle didn't continue with his tirade and chase him around the rear of the restaurant.

"It's okay, Joey. I'll buy you a new truck tomorrow," said Richie, calmly. His mind was already in motion as he deviously fingered pieces of the broken truck that were strewn about his workspace. "I know exactly what to do."

Minutes later Vinny was heading out of the kitchen to serve Mike his third plate of wings. The braggadocious college kid plowed into them with the same gusto as the first two flights, his friends hooting and hollering at the certainty of his victory. However, after Mike had only finished four of the wings, his pace began to drastically slow.

"What's wrong, kid? The wings a little too spicy for you?" asked Vinny, smiling. He was growing hopeful that Mike might not finish. He had seen this sort of thing before. Someone who was going strong on the challenge, quickly fade, and then beg for a glass of milk.

"C'mon, bro, you can take down these last six!" said Steve. "Let's go, Mike! Let's go, Mike!" He started thrusting his fist into the air and his pals joined in his chant.

Mike seemed to get a second wind then, downing another two wings, and then eating another, piece by piece. He was only three wings away from $1,000 and bragging rights.

"It's just not sitting in my stomach, right," said Mike. He had all but stopped eating by this point. "I'm gonna need a glass of..." Mike tumbled out of the booth, vomiting on himself and the floor.

"Ah, *shit*, dude," said Steve. "You were *so close!*"

Vinny felt a surge of relief as Mike hit the floor. He didn't know how his brother had done it, but Richie had once again delivered. "How much did he have to drink before he started eating?"

Steve and his friends had to lift Mike off the floor, as he was unresponsive to their shouts and slaps.

"Not much, man," said Steve, growing frightened at his friend's state. "Shit. I can hear his stomach gurgling!"

"Sick. We should call an ambulance," said another one of Mike's friends.

"No, no! Just drive him to the ER," said Vinny, trying to hush the guys from disturbing his other guests. A small crowd had already gathered to see what the commotion was. "Your food is on the house."

Steve and the guys liked the sound of that. They carried Mike out of the pub and took him to the hospital in Steve's car.

The emergency personnel took Mike right in and pumped his stomach after the guys told the doctor he had been in an eating contest. Mike eventually came to, then keeled over, complaining of a tremendous stomach pain.

"We'll give you a pain med, then place a camera into your stomach to have a look around while we're waiting for the test results from your stomach evacuation," said Dr. Ripert.

Not long after, Dr. Ripert was pushing a thin camera into Mike's mouth and down his esophagus. Mike was feeling better, quickly growing lightheaded from the opioid he had been given.

"Can you see those two small holes on the monitor?" asked Dr. Ripert.

"Are those, like, ulcers?" asked Mike.

"These are much worse than any ulcer I've ever seen," said Dr. Ripert. "You'll need surgery to repair these lesions, before morning."

Mike nodded, dumbly. "Did I get them tonight, from the hot sauce?"

"Oh, no. You've likely had these for some time," said Dr. Ripert, chuckling. "You don't get lesions like this from a few plates of Buffalo wings."

Just then, a nurse entered with the test results regarding the material pumped from Mike's stomach. The doctor looked over the report for a few minutes before he spoke. "Your results came back abnormal."

"Huh? What does that mean, Doc?"

"A significant amount of nickel-cadmium was detected."

"Okay...?"

"You've ingested battery acid, Mike," said Dr. Ripert. "You've been poisoned."

DANNY'S ROCK

"Dad, is this rock volcanic?" I asked, after discovering a strange, cratered rock. It was full of holes and about the size of a grapefruit.

My dad, Steve, took it from me for a closer look. "Yeah, this could be a large pumice stone, or maybe some other type of igneous rock," he said. "Although, the holes look a little big."

"I'm going to take it home and show Keith," I said. "He'll think it's cool." Keith was my older brother. He was thirteen and real popular at our junior high. He was old enough that he could choose to not to spend the weekend with our dad. It really hurt my dad's feelings when Keith turned him down most every weekend.

"Yeah, Keith will love it, buddy," he said. I felt bad for my dad. I was only eleven at the time, but I knew it was my mom's fault that they had split up. Now he only got to see us once a week, and he barely saw Keith. "Technically, we're not supposed to take anything off state land. But it's not a fossil, so I see no real harm in it."

"Cool!" I said. "Can we see the waterfall before we leave?"

"Sure, why not. We have time," he said.

We were hiking around Cascade Lake near my dad's house in Eagle Bay. I knew that when I turned thirteen

I'd still want to see him. We fished, hiked, canoed, camped, and even looked for ghosts together on Big Moose Lake. There was so much to do in the Adirondacks compared to my hometown of Utica.

Dad took some pictures of me posing by the waterfall. I even climbed up above and posed with a rock over my head like Link holding the Triforce in *The Legend of Zelda*.

We stopped at a diner in Old Forge on our way back to my mom's. I forgot about my rock while I downed chicken fingers and chatted with my dad about how the Yankees might do in the playoffs. I almost left it in my dad's Subaru, I was so tired by the time we got back to Utica.

"Danny, don't forget your pumice stone," Dad said.

My mom was outside. She had already grabbed my backpack and was guiding me toward the house. "Oh, real nice…" She made a face at the sight of the rock. It did look kind of gross with all its holes and the fact that it wasn't colorful, just a dull brown.

"Thanks, Dad," I said.

"I love you, buddy. Have a good week at school," he replied. "See you next week." He waved to Keith, who was standing in the window, watching. Keith didn't wave back.

"I love you, Dad. Bye." I watched him get back in his car and drive off. My parents had been divorced for over a year, but it still hurt to see him go.

"Hey, Keith. Check out my pumice stone." I held it out to him as soon as I came in and he snatched it up to investigate.

"Are you sure it's not a fossilized dinosaur turd? Because it looks like shit," said Keith, laughing.

"Keith Thomas Burr, you watch your mouth!" my mom said. She turned to me and asked if I wanted a Hot

Pocket. I declined. "Then go brush your teeth and get to bed. You have school in the morning."

I went to my room and unpacked my things. After I brushed my teeth I realized Keith still had my rock, so I went to his room. He was sitting in bed and he hid a magazine under his blanket when I came in.

"Knock first, dummy," said Keith.

I saw that my rock was sitting on his nightstand. I knew I could either try and grab it and run away, and hope that Mom might defend me in case he chased me; or I could ask for it back, in which case he'd probably make me pay him for it. I was tired, so I chose the latter.

"Hey, can I get my rock back?"

"I was thinking I might take it to school tomorrow and tell Kim Douglas it's a meteorite."

"Why?"

"Because she's a space case and she'll probably believe it," said Keith, smirking.

I knew it was going to be tough getting my rock back. I wasn't a snitch, and I knew Keith would really let me have it if I complained to Mom. "Okay. Can I have it back tomorrow after school?"

"Sure."

I sighed. I knew there was a fifty-fifty chance that he'd just toss it in the river after school the next day, just to see if it would float. "Next weekend me and Dad are camping on Stillwater. Remember the eighteen-inch bass you caught out there?"

"Have fun freezing your nuts off," said Keith.

"I thought it might be fun if you came with us..."

"I'm not going camping with Dad. He's a loser," said Keith. "He's way behind on his child support payments and Mom is having a tough time paying our bills."

"He has a new job. He'll catch up," I said. "It wasn't really fair of her to divorce him right when he got laid off, and then keep the house and everything…"

"Shut up! You have no idea what's going on," said Keith. "He's probably filling your head with all sorts of bullshit about Mom. That's exactly why I don't want to go camping with him. He'll say something nasty about Mom and I'd have to slap him for it."

"He doesn't say nasty things about Mom or anyone else. We had a good time…"

"Get out, dummy!"

I hurried back to my room and went to bed.

The following morning, while I was dragging my feet down the hall toward the bathroom, I thought about my special rock. Keith was a heavy sleeper and it took a major effort from Mom to wake him up and get him going. I thought I might try and steal my rock back and hide it from him.

I stopped in front of his closed bedroom door and listened. When I heard his heavy breathing, I knew he was sound asleep. So, I slowly opened his door and crept inside. There was plenty of light coming in from the partially open curtains, so I could see that my rock was still in the same place as the night before.

I tiptoed over to his nightstand and was about to snatch up the rock when I noticed a few small tubes emerging from the rock, extending to the pillow where my brother slept. They were squirming!

"Oh shit! *Mom!*" I screamed like a little kid, immediately waking Keith. He sat up, startled, and looked around, slowly assessing the situation.

"What the *hell* is wrong with you, dork?!"

I pointed at the writhing creatures on the nightstand and on his bed. I was shaking, horrified that they might be some form of alien life, that my rock was a fallen meteor.

Keith looked down and laughed as he swept the licorice-sized monstrosities off his pillow. "Sick. You found a worm rock..." He yawned before finishing his thought. I watched as a long, black worm tumbled from his mouth and onto his chin.

Keith's eyes went wide when he realized something was wriggling around on his bottom lip. He yanked it from his mouth, no longer amused. He then began to panic, contorting under his sheets as another emerged from one of his nostrils, then two more from his mouth, followed by one from his left ear...

FATHER-TO-BE

Mr. Schilling had nowhere else to go. Eighty-two years old and suffering from severe mobility issues brought on by diabetes and advanced emphysema, he could no longer safely live alone in his apartment. So, he reached out to his only living relative—his daughter, Elizabeth.

"You can stay with us, Dad." It was an agonizing decision for Elizabeth, as Mr. Schilling had subjected her to years of physical and emotional abuse. With the help of therapy and a supportive network of friends as an adult, Elizabeth had moved on, tucked it away, and finally made peace with her past.

But when Elizabeth asked her husband, Ben, if her ailing father could move into their two-bedroom apartment, Ben would have none of it. "He's been a cancer on your life from the beginning. I know you can't be happy under the same roof as him," said Ben. "I can't believe you're even considering this."

He knew the pain Mr. Schilling had inflicted on Elizabeth; she had wept in Ben's arms on more than one occasion when the subject of her childhood came up. For Ben, Mr. Schilling's abuse was unpardonable; he wanted nothing to do with the man, *let alone* share an apartment with him. To further complicate the issue, the couple was planning on having children soon. Not only did Benjamin detest Mr. Schilling, he thought it highly impractical to invite an elderly man into their home when they would need room for a child not far down the road.

"I'm all he's got left, Ben. The responsibility falls on me now," said Elizabeth, her voice tinged with doubt. "I just feel like it's my moral duty." As it happened with most arguments with his wife, Ben eventually capitulated, and Mr. Schilling soon moved in.

Almost immediately, the couple regretted their decision. Mr. Schilling was crusty, cantankerous, and displayed not a shred of gratitude to either of them. He moved into what the couple had planned on turning into a nursery, and it wasn't long before the room took on a musty, decaying odor. The aura of Mr. Schilling permeated the entire living space, the hallways, the living room. When he wasn't collecting dust in his bed, he lurched around the apartment with his walker, in his robe and slippers, coughing, sometimes wetting the couple's plush beige couch.

"Lizzie, I know I'm on my way out," said Mr. Schilling. "But do I have to sit in my own piss puddle all afternoon?!"

Time that Ben and Elizabeth might have spent together was entirely eaten up by the sour old man and his near-constant demands. Mr. Schilling always needed something: pills, food, coffee, diapers. Ben worked long days at an investment bank and it infuriated him to have to give up what little free time he had tending to the man. Mr. Schilling was a monster of a houseguest, and always the memory of his past deeds hung heavy in the air. And even though Ben knew the feeble man could no longer physically harm Elizabeth, he had witnessed the way in which Mr. Schilling could still mesmerize his daughter, almost as if the old man could tap into the young girl which lay dormant inside her.

Ben would often walk by Mr. Schilling's room and look in as he slept. This man who had brought so much torment on his wife, sleeping soundly in a cushy apartment, his every need tended to. Mr. Schilling was weak, vulnerable, and Ben often wondered how easy it would be to walk in some night and put an end to his and Elizabeth's tormentor with nothing more than a pillow.

But Ben knew that Mr. Schilling likely only had months to live. So, he waited it out, optimistic that with each day Elizabeth's father drew one step closer to death. At which point they could reclaim their home and work on building the family they had always imagined for themselves, putting this unwelcome situation behind them.

One evening, Ben came home from work to hear the unmistakable sound of Elizabeth weeping. When he got to the bedroom hallway, Ben found her leaving Mr. Schilling's room.

"Honey, what's wrong?" asked Ben.

"Nothing," said Elizabeth, sniffling. Her face was wet with tears.

"Nothing? You're a mess, Liz. What happened?"

She paused, gathering her thoughts. "It's just hard having him around. I can't erase the memories, Ben, no matter how hard I try. And it's been rough taking care of him. It's rough on us."

Ben nodded. "I know. Liz, it's like we haven't had a moment together since he moved in."

"We haven't made love in a while either," said Elizabeth, softly. "Remember our plans? The baby..."

Ben took her hand and led her to their bedroom for some privacy.

As Mr. Schilling's health continued to deteriorate, his attitude only worsened. He shouted at Ben and Elizabeth, criticizing their home, the food, the way they lived, staring at them with his penetrating, grey eyes, judging. The couple had made a promise to spend more time together, but they found it increasingly difficult to do so. Even when they could find a spare hour, they were often too stressed to think about such things as intimacy or romance.

However, after months of heartache and crushing anxiety, there would be some light in the darkness. The couple was overjoyed when Elizabeth discovered that she was pregnant. But the excitement of the pregnancy was almost immediately eclipsed by Mr. Schilling. He fell while walking to the bathroom, which only exacerbated his deteriorating condition.

Ben and Elizabeth had to spend even more time tending to his needs, ensuring that he was well-hydrated and that he received pain medication multiple times a day. The weeks and months became even more difficult for the expecting family. Baby clothes needed to be purchased, Lamaze classes had been booked, but serving as Mr. Schilling's live-in caretakers left them no time to tend to their own needs.

When Elizabeth reached her eighth month of pregnancy, she was no longer able to care for her father; Ben now bore the bulk of the duties. He had avoided cleaning up Mr. Schilling after his bowel movements, but the job now fell solely on him. To perform such a task for a man so reprehensible infuriated Ben to no end. As he cleaned Mr. Schilling, Ben noticed an odd-looking birthmark behind the man's ear. It was shaped like a star, almost symmetrical, and Ben nearly mistook it for a tattoo. Ben's attention was pulled away from the strange mark when Mr. Schilling shouted at him for wiping him too roughly. Ben quickly finished the job and left the bathroom in a fit.

Ben had finally reached his breaking point. He had complained about the man to Elizabeth here and there—he didn't want to upset his wife in her third trimester—but he could hold back no longer. They shared a moment alone together in the kitchen, both breaking down in tears.

"The man barked at me while I was wiping his goddamn ass!" said Ben, making no attempt to conceal his feelings from the man lying in the other room. "I know he's your father, but dammit, Liz, I can only take so much."

"I know, Ben," said Elizabeth, lowering herself onto the couch. She had put on 30 pounds and was nearly as immobile as her father. "Just please, hold on a little longer. You see how bad he's getting."

"I don't care how old he is or how much pain he's in. He shouldn't say the things he does. The physical abuse might've stopped years ago, but he's still the same old, vile insect of a man..." Ben cringed, as his wife began to cry uncontrollably.

That night, Ben snuck out of bed and crept down the hallway. He stopped outside Mr. Schilling's room and cracked the door open. A small sliver of light landed on the bed, revealing the man's shape under the blankets. His back was to the door, and Ben could see the elderly man's head in the scant light, including the birthmark behind his ear.

Mr. Schilling's breathing was labored. His lean body was lost in the bulk of the blankets. Were he any other man in such a condition, he would have engendered some sympathy, but Ben knew the vile creature that inhabited that withered frame. It was his knowledge of his father-in-law's true nature, and the rage that had built up inside him since his introduction to their home, that drove him to approach the bed. Without forethought, Ben picked up a spare pillow and held it down over Mr. Schilling's head. He heard the slightest of groans through the feather and cotton, and felt his father-in-law kick weakly, futilely, beneath him. As life began to leave the old man, Ben considered his unborn son and the space he would eventually occupy. He drew back at the thought of christening his son's room with a murder.

Ben lifted the pillow from Mr. Schilling and looked for signs of life. The man lay still, so Ben slapped his cheek and shook him by the shoulder until the man croaked. Ben hurried out of the room, relieved. His heart raced as he looked in the hall mirror, wide-eyed. He shivered when he heard an uncanny wheeze and gasping from the room he had just exited. The noise had startled Elizabeth awake and Ben followed her as she made her way into Mr. Schilling's room, where the man lay in bed, the left side of his face drooping, babbling something incomprehensible. Elizabeth frantically threw the blankets off and tended to her father, shouting at Ben to call an ambulance.

As he made the phone call, Ben looked on, astonished that the old man had survived but somewhat satisfied that he was, justly, suffering. An emergency medical crew arrived at the apartment and Mr. Schilling was rushed to Binghampton General.

"Your father's had a stroke and is recovering in intensive care," said the doctor who approached Ben and Elizabeth in the waiting area. "He is in stable condition. You can see him now."

Ben, dazed, nodded to the man. How many more months, or years, would this scumbag live? He could only imagine how much more care his father-in-law would now require.

The couple were led to a room in the ICU, where Mr. Schilling lay. Never had he looked more vulnerable. To the hospital staff, Mr. Schilling likely appeared a pitiable old man, a grandfather-to-be under great duress, but Ben knew better.

Mr. Schilling was conscious but unable to speak. Elizabeth stood silent in the doorframe. One lazy eye followed Ben from the door to the side of his bed. The old man's eyeball then rolled back in its socket, his only defense against his would-be murderer. Ben had felt prisoner in his own home, but now felt a kind of power over Mr. Schilling, seeing that he frightened him.

"Excuse me, sir."

Ben tensed at the sound of a woman's voice behind him. He turned to see a nurse, pushing a wheeled monitor toward the bed.

"Sorry," said Ben, allowing her by.

The woman spoke to her patient. "My name is Betty. I'll be looking after you. Can you understand me, Mr. Schilling?"

The broken old man managed a slight groan. His working eye darted to Ben and then the nurse, back and forth. Ben felt confident that Mr. Schilling would be unable to point him out as his attacker, yet the old man's one-eyed gaze weighed on him. *Maybe they'll figure it out*, he thought. *Maybe Schilling will be able to communicate with them.*

Ben left the room and waited in the hall. He could hear Elizabeth gently talking to her father. It was 2 A.M. when they returned home to their apartment. Elizabeth found it difficult to sleep, as she was quite shaken by the night's events.

Ben was awoken at dawn by a guttural cry. He sat up in bed and saw Elizabeth clutching herself, the stress of the night triggering early labor. For the second time in less than 12 hours, they hurried to the hospital.

Hours later, Elizabeth lie screaming in the delivery room, her face glistening with sweat. Soon she was pushing out a baby boy.

"He's here, Ben," said Elizabeth, weakly but smiling.

"I know, honey. He's beautiful," said Ben.

After cleaning the baby, a nurse carried him over to the couple, resting him on Elizabeth's breast.

Ben, in his newfound bliss, allowed himself to breathe. The burden of Mr. Schilling was forgotten in that moment, and he and Elizabeth finally had what they long dreamt of. It was when Ben picked up his son and proudly inspected his soft, pink body, that he saw it. A birthmark behind the boy's ear. A carbon copy of his father-in-law's star-shaped blemish.

Ben yelped and inadvertently jostled the baby in his hands, causing his son to cry. He handed him back to Elizabeth, pointing behind the boy's ear. "The birthmark!"

"Yes, just like Daddy's." Elizabeth soothed the newborn in her arms. "Isn't he amazing?"

Ben blanched at the connection between the terrible old man and his new son. "It's okay. We can get it removed."

"Oh, no. Daddy wouldn't like that."

Ben recoiled at her regressive, childlike tone.

"What do you mean?" He felt a terrible aching deep in his stomach, recalling the entranced, otherworldly state in which he had found his wife after returning home from work early, from time to time, or having found her late at night in the hallway, between the bedrooms. The birthmark. Either alone, curious, passed over without analysis; now unmistakably, a sickening connective tissue beyond coincidence...

Nurse Betty then entered with Mr. Schilling's doctor, interrupting Ben's uncomfortable conversation with his wife. The pair broke the news that Elizabeth's father had peacefully slipped away within the hour.

"It's too bad your father isn't here to see this," said the nurse, admiring the brand-new family. "But I'm sure he would be proud."

Ben looked to his wife as he stood beside the bed, trembling, fearful of her sudden change in character.

"Oh, but he *is* here," stated Elizabeth, as she gazed into the eyes of her baby boy.

THE DEVIL'S CABIN

My friend Adam and I rented a cabin in early July at Letchworth State Park in New York. We wanted to see its massive gorges and picturesque waterfalls for ourselves, after hearing so much about this so-called 'Grand Canyon of the East.' During our visit we drove through and hiked much of the seventeen-mile-long park, and it certainly lived up to its hype—however we only ended up staying one night at our cabin.

The 'D Cabins' are a small grouping of one-room lodges in the southeastern quarter of the park. They are in a remote area of Letchworth, in that most tourists and hikers congregate on the western side of the Genesee River Gorge. Adam and I were practically alone in the congregation of eight or so cabins when we arrived. A man and a woman from a neighboring cabin were packing up to leave as we were unpacking our car, and they kindly handed us a watermelon before they left. They seemed to be in a hurry, so we didn't chat with them for very long. Once they were gone there were only two other occupied cabins, but they were distant enough from us that we never really saw much of those people during our night's stay. We didn't hang around the cabin long once the car was unloaded.

We were on our way to a trailhead when we spotted a Civil War parade field with a cannon and memorial. It was strange seeing an empty field and barren picnicking area in a popular state park in July, so I commented that the field must be haunted by Civil War ghosts. Adam suggested that we should revisit it some night and see for ourselves.

The hike itself was fun. We found our way down to the river canyon and eventually crossed over to the western side and saw one of the waterfalls.

When we returned to our cabin that evening it was already twilight. We played a few board games, ate sandwiches, then put down our folding cots. The cabin was basically the size of a kitchen. It had a small stove and refrigerator, a tiny table with two chairs, and two rolling cots. Once they were down, it was difficult to move anywhere. Scratched into the log walls were countless names and dates of past occupants; friends, lovers, and vandals all made their presence known, some from as far back as the 1970s. We weren't the sort of people to carve our names into a cabin.

"Look at that—a pentagram," said Adam.

I went over and inspected the star. There were some symbols I didn't recognize around it. It stood out because every other carving seemed to either be an expression of love, something lewd, or a record of someone's presence. "Great, we're staying in the Devil's Cabin," I said, jokingly.

Adam shrugged it off and we moved on. We eventually sat down for a round of cards and had a few drinks.

"Hey, how about we cut that watermelon open?" said Adam.

"With what?" I asked. There was not cutlery of any kind in the cabin.

"Good question," said Adam. "I think I have my pocket knife in my bag."

He retrieved his Swiss Army-style knife, and it took about fifteen minutes with the small blade struggling to cut through the rind, but eventually we were able to pry the melon into halves.

"Nasty," said Adam as we revealed the black, gooey rot which had consumed the melon.

The molded innards began to run onto the floor from my half. It seemed to have liquified as soon as it was exposed to the air. "Quick, toss it!"

We both heaved our portions of the stinking, sopping mess out the cabin door and into the woods. It was a unique rot—a sweet, fetid decomposition.

Adam and I cleaned up the floor and laughed at the 'gift' our neighbors had left us. We then returned to our game, but soon enough we were nodding off, and eventually agreed that it was time for bed. It was still relatively early, but it was dark, and we were beat from a full day of hiking.

I fell asleep immediately and slept for hours, before I was rudely awakened by a knock at the cabin door. Honestly, it was more of a rumbling—like someone was shaking the door as opposed to knocking it. Darkness had enveloped the cabin, inside and out, and I couldn't hear much of anything with the small fan that was blowing in the window, only a yard or so from my head. I got up, looked to Adam, who was still sleeping, then checked my phone for the time. It was 2:30 a.m.

It was an eerie feeling, the uncertainty of who was at the door at that hour. I was tense, though not yet scared, as I had been camping a time or two when a ranger or park attendant had interrupted my night's sleep for various reasons. Sometimes it was because someone was missing in the area, and sometimes it was for maddening reasons, like two tents were too close to each other, even though we had rented two adjoining campsites, so we could camp together.

I flipped the outside light on and unlocked the door, then slowly cracked it open to look out. I was in my boxers and a T-shirt, so I immediately felt self-conscious when I saw that it was an old woman out there.

"Can I help you?" I asked. I couldn't get a good look at her face, as it was mostly obscured by the dark. She had a hunchback and her long, scraggly grey hair was tucked into a green Army jacket.

She then held up something and I realized she was offering it to me. "I have an extra cantaloupe. Would you like it?"

I didn't immediately reply, as I was floored by how rude she had been to wake me up so early in the morning to offer me a cantaloupe. I assumed she was crazy, and wanted to get back to bed, so I simply said that I would take her melon. I cracked the door enough to reach out and receive the fruit.

"Enjoy," she said.

I thanked her and closed the door. I peeked out of the window to make sure she was leaving, and once she drifted off into the night I turned off the outside light, tossed the cantaloupe onto the stove and went back to bed. I couldn't get back to sleep, as I pictured the old crone watching the cabin from somewhere close by.

I thought of the unsolved Keddie Murders, a family who were gruesomely murdered one night at a cabin in California. A couple of children were left unharmed in another room and had slept through the brutal slayings, and no one who was staying in any of the neighboring cabins had heard anything either. I wondered if Adam would have woken up if the old woman had stabbed me through the door, as opposed to handing me a melon.

There were a few mosquitoes and moths in the cabin now, so I was also having real and imagined encounters with them, which prolonged my sleeplessness. And I couldn't quite stretch my legs, as I would touch the walls and didn't like the idea of creepy crawlies having easy access to me. But I was still tired, so eventually, I drifted back off to sleep.

I'm not sure how long I slept, but it wasn't yet dawn, as everything was still incredibly dark. But I was awakened again, this time more gradually, by a man's voice in the area. I couldn't understand what he was saying at first, and I figured he was some distance away. But when I got up to peek out the window, I quickly realized that someone was standing just outside the door. I couldn't quite make him out, but I could hear that he was talking low—not quite whispering but speaking in hushed tones. The fan made it difficult to understand what he was saying, but it felt too weird, and was too much of an unknown to just confront him— so I woke Adam up.

"What?!" Adam's eye went wide in the miniscule amount of light that came in from the moon and the bathroom building which was just down the road.

"It sounds like some guy outside the cabin is talking to himself."

"Huh? What time is it?" He sat up, seeming to understand that I was scared, and this was some sort of situation.

"After three, maybe a little after four. I don't know," I said. "An old lady came by about an hour ago and knocked on the door. Now this guy's out there."

"Turn on the light."

I got up and leaned over the table and flipped on both switches. One illuminated the inside of the cabin and the other the outside. Adam got up and went to the door, cracking it.

"What's going on? Why are you here so late?"

Adam blocked my view outside, so I couldn't see who he was talking to. "No. We don't want that," he stated. "We want to get some rest; it's the middle of the night."

I heard a response, but couldn't make out what was said, then Adam closed the door.

"What did he want?"

Adam flipped the outside light off. He turned to me and I noticed that his face had lost much of its color. He was looking past me when he spoke. "It wasn't a man, it was an old lady."

I could've sworn I'd heard a man talking out there. The old woman I'd spoken to earlier hadn't sounded like a man. "Was she wearing a green jacket?"

"Yep. I assume it's the same old bag."

"She gave me this cantaloupe..." I didn't finish my thought, as when I turned to the stove to retrieve the melon, I found it cracked and covered in a dark mold, with tiny worms and larvae swarming over it.

"That's nasty, dude," said Adam, nearly retching when he saw it. "Why would you bring that in here?"

"It wasn't like that when I took it..." I grabbed a plastic shopping bag and picked up the disgusting cantaloupe, opened the door and tossed it outside. I locked the door and we huddled over the table.

"What did she say to you?" I asked. "I couldn't really hear over the fan."

"She said something about having lived in this cabin during the off-season. Then she tried to hand me a knife..."

"*What?!*"

"I know. She wanted me to take the knife. She said I didn't have one big enough to cut my friend's melon..."

We stayed awake and vigilant until dawn, thankfully without any further visitations. As soon as there was enough light, we packed up the car and left the cabin village. We had no intention of staying another night at the 'Devil's Cabin.'

ACKNOWLEDGEMENTS

Special thanks to Chad Wehrle, for designing a cover that embodies the tone of this collection (see you back for Volume 3!) Burt Myers for helping us with additional design elements. Sybil, Emily, and our children for their encouragement and inspiration. And as always, Zinger (may he RIP in Peace.)

**Make sure to check out these other books
by Brhel & Sullivan...**

Tales from Valleyview Cemetery
Marvelry's Curiosity Shop
At the Cemetery Gates: Year One
Carol for a Haunted Man
Corpse Cold: New American Folklore
Her Mourning Portrait and Other Paranormal Oddities
Resurrection High

31062761R00105

Made in the USA
Columbia, SC
01 November 2018